Praise for F

'Exceptional stories, stay with you. A true celebration of the short-story form.'
Huma Qureshi

'As a short-story writer and reader, I don't need much convincing of the special power of the form, but these entries confirmed it once more – and most emphatically!'
Wendy Erskine

'An illuminating and vivid range of stories from an exciting array of new voices already so accomplished in their craft.'
Sharmaine Lovegrove

'I really appreciate the range and ambition on display in these stories. These are writers putting work into voice and craft rather than relying on event alone, and that's what makes their work persist in the mind.'
Chris Power

'One of the best multi-author short-story collections that I have read in recent years.'
Jarred McGinnis

'Testament to the breadth and imagination of a new generation of writers, and the elasticity of the short-story form.'
Anne Meadows

'A joy to discover these fresh voices in fiction.'
Elise Dillsworth

'This anthology presents a thrilling sample of distinctive

new talent at work today and highlights some exciting emerging writers for us all to follow.'

Kishani Widyaratna

'The stories on this longlist showcase the range and excitement of the form.'

Chris Wellbelove

'A formally inventive and consistently surprising patchwork of stories. This wide-ranging collection shows how elastic the short-story form is, and these writers are pulling it in exciting new directions.'

Gurnaik Johal

'Full of verve, emotional enquiry and imagination.'

Harriet Moore

'An amazingly diverse list. All the stories have their own unique energy, originality and power.'

Zoe Gilbert

'Eclectic, accomplished, bursting with life – an act of literature in discovery.'

Kit Caless

'Arrives and lands with thrilling confidence, quickly establishing an atmosphere that is subtle but indelible.'

Emma Paterson, on the 2019 winner

'Full of different voices, experimentations with language and storytelling and with different approaches to evoking imagery and reaction.'

Melissa Cox

'An energising array of short stories, with an abundance of ambition and talent on display.'

Kiya Evans

Brick Lane Bookshop
New Short Stories 2024

A BLB Press Publication

First published by BLB Press in 2024
Copyright of the Individual Authors, 2024

All rights reserved.

No part of this publication may be reproduced, stored in a retrieval system, or transmitted, in any form or by any means, without the prior permission in writing of the publisher, nor be otherwise circulated in any form of binding or cover other than that in which it is published and without a similar condition including this condition being imposed on the subsequent publisher.

ISBN 978-1-9162082-5-4

BLB Press Ltd
Brick Lane Bookshop
166 Brick Lane
London
E1 6RU

www.bricklanebookshop.org

A CIP record for this book is available from the British Library

Printed and bound in Great Britain by Clays Ltd, Elcograf S.p.A.

Designed, typeset and project-managed by Kate Ellis

to the power of independent booksellers

Contents

Foreword, Denise Jones	ix
Introduction, Kate Ellis	xiii
Menagerie, Jane Coneybeer	1
Un, Louie Conway	19
The Birth of a Devil Sheep, David McGrath	37
Green, Laura Surynt	49
The Second Can Wait, Sharmaine Lim	61
A Love Story, Karishma Jobanputra	81
Keiko and I, Rosie Chen	97
Heroes of the South West, Ali Roberts	115
Glue, Danny Beusch	137
DAIRY FARM RAIDED BY GIANT BIRD, Sukie Wilson	149
Fool's Gold, Sean Bell	159
Aqua Vitae, Karrish Devan	169
Contributors' Bios	179
Judges' Bios	183
Judges' Quotes	185
Writers' Endorsements	191
Thanks	195

Foreword

Denise Jones

I hope you enjoy this collection, the sixth *Brick Lane Bookshop New Short Stories* anthology, composed of the longlist of stories by new writers entered for the 2024 Short Story Prize. Huge congratulations to the winners and many thanks to the judges, the readers, the copy-editor and the BLB Press staff, Kate, Olly, Jo, Polly and Bret, who manage the competition so brilliantly. Based on the success of this venture, Brick Lane Bookshop now hosts writers' workshops, which are proving to be tremendously popular.

We're happy to be celebrating our twentieth anniversary on Brick Lane this year, 2024, and also to be remembering that the bookshop has a rich history which goes back forty-six years. Founded in 1978, the shop has served the community of East London with dedication and passion, and by championing independent enterprises and writers. It began in the East End as a community-based Tower Hamlets Arts Project (THAP) initiative, THAP Books, and was started in response to the absence of bookshops in the area, which one high-street retailer wrongly attributed to the idea that the 'people in the East End didn't read'!

A group of like-minded people, including myself, opened the bookshop and arts project in Watney Street, Shadwell, and moved to larger premises on Whitechapel Road in 1980. In 1994 we changed the names to Eastside Books and Eastside Arts Wordcentre and ran a literature-based community arts programme until the lease on the premises ended in 2004, when it was decided to wind everything down. Details of this history are on the bookshop website.

With the passionate belief that the area still needed a bookshop, I took a financial risk, found an empty shop in Brick Lane and moved the bookshop there from Whitechapel, finally changing the name to Brick Lane Bookshop in 2018. Due to a brilliant and talented staff team, the shop has grown from strength to strength. Each member of staff who has joined us has brought different skills that have added to the activities the shop can provide our customers.

We offer a varied range of literature, support independent presses, run a vibrant author events programme, and we're committed to working with our community to nurture a love of reading from a young age. We're excited about working with local schools and have started a Young Readers' Fund to provide books for children whose families can't afford to buy any. Since its inception, Brick Lane Bookshop has served as a cultural hub and continues this legacy through its East End Writers' Workshop, Reading East London group, and the flagship Short Story Prize. In 2019 we set up a publishing company, BLB Press Ltd, to run the competition and to publish the longlist of twelve stories. The press also publishes a literary newsletter, *the blb*, which invites submissions, and other publications are in the pipeline.

We have shown how independent bookshops are integral to fostering community links through promoting East London history and literature with walks, talks and cabaret evenings, and the community has demonstrated an insatiable appetite for books and the magic of storytelling. We're happy to draw in huge crowds of tourists and locals alike, who come for the wide selection of books and proceed to carry our iconic tote bags around the world.

Our twentieth year on Brick Lane looks just as promising as the previous nineteen. We're delighted to have been named the London Regional Winner of Independent Bookshop of the Year at the 2024 British Book Awards, which recognise and celebrate the outstanding contributions of bookshops across the UK. Amid stiff competition the judges commented that the shop stood out for its unwavering commitment to building a literary community and championing diverse voices in literature.

Now that some local authorities have been forced to close libraries, and, nationally, one in seven primary schools don't have a school library, independent bookshops are becoming increasingly important on the high street. At Brick Lane Bookshop we try our best to support distinct voices and emerging authors, stock both mainstream and independent publications, and encourage new writing by sponsoring the Short Story Prize.

For more detailed information about Brick Lane Bookshop and BLB Press, see our website www.bricklanebookshop.org.

Denise Jones
Owner Brick Lane Bookshop Ltd
August 2024

Introduction

Kate Ellis

In your hands are twelve new short stories by writers you have probably not heard of before. To get here, they were selected from over one thousand entries to the 2024 Brick Lane Bookshop Short Story Prize, read anonymously by three rounds of different readers and chosen for their quality, rawness, experimentation and originality. This anthology is a wild, emotional, difficult, surprising and, at times, funny read. Put together, the characters in this book would make a horrifically awkward but utterly fascinating dinner party. The clear-up would take days and leave many questions.

Walking to the launch party for last year's anthology, I was unsure how and whether to continue running the short story prize. I'd been working on it mainly solo since 2019 but had become too busy to carry on and had no idea how to hand it over, or to whom.

The weather was ferocious that night – warnings of disruptions and dangerous winds, perhaps even leaves on train tracks (!) – but the bookshop was packed. Most of the longlisted writers were able to come, and many brought friends, family and supporters. The readings were wonderful and the winner announcement was met with a delighted roar. There was a proper buzz in the air, a warm atmosphere, an excited energy. It reminded me what the competition was for, and that publishing new writers matters. It changes perspectives, gives validation, raises hope.

By the end of the event, I was convinced the short story prize should continue. It took a few more months to figure out exactly how to share the contents of my head and laptop, but I did and now the competition is run by a small team of Brick Lane booksellers, who have organised and improved it already. I'm extremely grateful for the hard work of Jo, Olly and Polly, and, as ever, for the unwavering support of Brick Lane Bookshop's owner, Denise Jones. The competition is entirely funded by the bookshop, a small but mighty independent. The attitude has always been to prioritise interesting projects and community, which means we can keep the prize going for as long as there are new writers to discover, publish and celebrate.

This year, we're fortunate to have three brilliant literary brains as prize judges: Dan Bird, an editor at Granta; Lucy Luck, of C&W literary agency; and Vanessa Onwuemezi, author of *Dark Neighbourhood*. They had the unenviable task of deciding the winning stories and shortlist of six. All three praised the high quality of the entire longlist and along the way, stories were compared to Elena Ferrante, Jez Butterworth and Tobias Wolff, and described as moving, skilful, breathless, tense, strange, comical, brilliant, engaging, claustrophobic, sharp and fun.

In this book, you will encounter a distracted babysitter, voracious consumption in New York, late-life transformation, a stamp fetish, an infamous motherfucker, the releasing of spirits in a hospice, a blizzard-whipped restaurant, OnlyFans, post-natal trauma, a teenage wordsmith, fecund foliage and a flooded world. There's a lot going on. This is not a hug of a book, nor is it traditional beach reading, but there's plenty of that out there. Small presses exist to publish what's on the peripheries, the writers the mainstream may not take a chance on, especially so early in their careers. This is a slice of short-story writing in the UK right now, a taster of fresh talent to watch out for.

Here's to keeping going, to longevity, to the endless excitement of discovering new writers, new stories and new voices. To the joy of reading, writing, exploring on the page and enduring storms. I hope you enjoy the ride. Thanks for reading.

Kate Ellis
Project Manager Brick Lane Bookshop Short Story Prize
August 2024

Brick Lane Bookshop

New Short Stories 2024

Menagerie

Jane Coneybeer

On the first day, they bring me water in a glass cup – a real glass cup, not one of the shitty plastic sippy cups they make the dying drink from – and there's even an ice cube, *an ice cube*, that floats and floats until it's winnowed away by the warmth of my palms. The danger of choking recedes. I drink the stale water and the glass is taken.

'Would you like a facility tour?' the nurse asks. It's a formality. Her nose is long, curved, beak-like. Her voice is piercing. Her scrubs are like plumage, tropical green and blue and yellow. The name on her tag is bolded and large and unreadable.

'That would be wonderful,' my mother says, because I'm staring at this woman who might grow wings at any moment. And of course we'd like a facility tour, who wouldn't, that would be simply absurd. My mother touches my elbow, gently, like testing a roll of fly tape in the summer, and I stick.

'Sure,' I agree, because I was raised to be polite.

'It's only temporary,' my mother reassures me. 'Then you'll come home. Of course.'

'Of course.' I am her echo.

I'm drifting, barely touching the ground: a new treatment, a surgery, has been proposed. That small word, *surgery*, is a life raft. Insurance will cover it; this is a temporary hospice stay. A respite. I read the pamphlets, over and over and over again until the words are etched into the folds of my treacherous brain.

Respite: a short period of rest or relief from something difficult or unpleasant.

At night in the weeks prior to my arrival here, whispers behind closed doors at my mother's house, where I swore never to live again. A woman's voice: 'Longer than expected . . .', and a man: '. . . inevitable.' Unconcealed sobs. Tiptoeing down the stairs, keeping to the sides so they don't creak. I am an object of shame. I am an object of pain. I am an object from which one desires respite.

'Here's the kitchen,' the bird woman says. Inside, a dog stands on its hind legs and leans against the counter. One, two, three, it rolls back and forth. Impossibly prehensile paws cling to a rolling pin. One, two, three. The motion is hypnotic. A shark, circling behind him. There's blood in the water.

'Oh,' I say. 'I do like baking.'

'Wonderful,' my mother repeats. 'Isn't it just wonderful?'

'We're always looking for ways to keep you engaged,' the nurse tells me, *me*, not my mother.

'Mallory has wonderful recipes,' she says anyways.

Wonderful, wonderful, *wonderful*.

Wonderful: inspiring delight, pleasure, or admiration. Extremely good. Marvellous.

'I do like baking,' I say. Dying is not wonderful. A respite stay is not wonderful. Nothing about the past year of my life has felt wonderful. But, because I know I've repeated myself and that's one of the *acute signs of mental deterioration*, I add, 'I taught my younger brother.'

'Your mother told me you have a large family,' the nurse says. We're moving again. The halls are short, the doors infinite. This is a sterile and sinking ship.

'Yeah.'

'They can come visit, of course. And there're rooms where they can spend the night.' She's relentless, this songbird. She's sung this tune a thousand times.

The furniture creaks when I test each couch cushion, each chair. I scoot from place to place and they watch. I am on exhibit. It's all new. Expensive. I sit on the floor and watch the motion of the waves. Back and forth, the room sways. I trace the pattern on the blue carpet.

'It's only temporary,' the songbird chirps to my mother. 'I've heard excellent things about Dr Brumm.'

'I only worry . . .'

'Of course.'

I get up. 'How old is this . . .' The word – it should start with an 'F', I know because she said it five minutes ago – is gone. 'Place?'

Songbird beams at my interest. 'Two years.'

'Are there ghosts?'

She's taken aback.

'I mean to ask,' I continue, because I've always wanted to live somewhere haunted, 'how many people have died here?'

'Mallory!' My mother is not pleased.

'It's perfectly normal to wonder,' Songbird assures her. 'Although medical records are confidential. I'm not allowed to tell you, I'm afraid.'

She's *afraid*. She has no idea.

'I imagine you and Cynthia will get along well.' Songbird's smile doesn't meet her eyes. 'She's one of our grief counsellors.'

'So, a lot, then?' I can't meet her eyes. The walls are painted eggshell white. It used to be my favourite colour. A contrarian colour. A grown-up colour. Warmly uncaring. I look out a floor-length window to the enrichment yard. A tiger pushes around a pumpkin filled with ground beef. A grizzled old elephant sits on a bench in the shade, staring at the sky.

In the silence, I insist, 'I just want to know if there are ghosts.'

My mother clears her throat.

Songbird doesn't answer.

I continue: 'Ten, twenty? If there are more than thirty, God help us all.'

'We have game nights on Tuesday, and movie nights on Friday.' Songbird is heroic in her effort to change the subject. 'To accommodate families that want to visit.'

Want to visit.

My mother's hand reaches for mine. I take it, like I'm a child again, and it's comforting and creased and old, so old, and I think that this woman must be ancient. I release her hand when I can't bear the warmth any longer and she clenches it into a fist, knuckles turning white as she presents a tearless face to the hospice.

Songbird opens a cabinet and the board games gleam

like a treasure trove, achingly familiar and painfully clinical. There are no missing Monopoly pieces. The playing cards still have their jokers. I imagine pressing the sanded Scrabble tiles against the pale undersides of my forearms until the letters are a part of me. I hold a white knight in my clammy fingers and don't let go.

'I want a Ouija board,' I tell my mother.

On the third day, I write on the whiteboard beside my door: 'DORM LIVIN''. I try to draw myself but all I can muster is a stick figure with too many arms and legs, frazzled hair, and black dots for eyes. The air conditioning pumps dry air in and out, iron lungs breathing for the building. I've decided that it isn't haunted, after all. Nobody would want to linger here with unfinished business when they can move on to the great void beyond. It's too lifeless.

'I AM IN PRISON', I write below the first line. It almost rhymes. I erase it with a finger, chew on the end of the marker. It's a lie. I can leave at any time. My spider-self hangs on a silken line. 'MY BODY IS A PRISON', I try. Still not right. There's a black smudge beneath 'DORM LIVIN''. I leave it alone for now.

When Songbird comes to wake me, I'm already up. The sea was too restless. She applauds my creativity. Today, she wears pink and yellow. She's a walking lemonade stand. She offers to get me more colours, to give my drawing more life.

'Can you give me more life?' I ask.

Songbird titters and chirps and says something meaningless and I take the offered dry erase markers and draw the first thing I can think of, an enormous penis, in the middle of the black smudge, neon colours blending into an earthy and unrecognisable muddle.

My family arrives as a howling pack and I'm caught up in hugs and kisses and tangible affection, foreign affection, sloppy affection. A pair of bear cubs cling to my legs. A dog and a hyena raise their noses to the air and sniff with exaggerated care, inhaling the smell of convalescence. I'm wrapped in a feathery embrace. I'm amazed that this many animals are allowed inside the building. I'm certain the sound can be heard from miles away.

I show them my room. They're easily impressed. It's *wonderful*. They've brought double-sided tape and printed photos of our family all together. I put them above my desk, where I can see them from my bed, and then we go to the common room and watch *Pirates of the Caribbean*, the third one, the worst one, which drags on and on and on, droning in the background, and the whole time, while my siblings roll around on the floor and give side-eye to my fellow *wonderful* respite patients, I'm considering throwing the Scrabble board across the room to hear the pieces hit the window.

My mother opens with 'HEALTH'. She asks, 'How're you settling in?'

'Fine,' I say. There's ink on my fingertips. 'How long until surgery?'

'A week.' She looks away. I get the feeling that I've already asked. She plays 'MENAGERIE', building on my meagre 'HEART' and 'WATER'. It's a Scrabble bingo, all seven tiles played at once. Double score. Seventy-four points.

If I put a tile in my mouth, will it dissolve? I want to

test my theory, but we're in public and that would upset my mother, so instead I play 'ZEALOT'.

'It isn't haunted here after all,' I say. Seventy points. It makes 'AT' and 'ZA'. We debate whether 'ZA' is a word. The pages of the Scrabble dictionary sigh; open, closed. 'This place is soulless.'

'A little,' she agrees. Her tiles spell out 'OXY' and 'WATERY' for seventy-five points. The numbers seem impossibly large. I think we're scoring the game wrong.

'ME'. Ten points, just out of spite.

Seven days. My whiteboard has been erased again.

Inoperable, they said. The MRI showed the leeching tendrils in my brain. They have me in a chokehold. *Accelerated growth*, they said. A promising new treatment is years too late to rescue me. I am adrift. The doctor prescribed something new for the pain. I'm given a timeframe that doesn't matter. There will be no surgery. There is no life raft.

My mother doesn't cry. She never cries in public.

In a private grief counselling session, I try to explain that I'm making art like the walls of Lascaux, that I'm creating a liminal space from which all things will be reborn, that I am the mother goddess who heralds divine creation.

A 'V' is carved with care at the entrance. The animals all face outwards. They stampede towards the light. Their spirits yearn for release, are granted peace through remembrance. In the darkest chamber, deep within a womb of earth and stone, Songbird is the bird-headed shaman and Cynthia the bison who has been speared. They are dying together within me.

'Why not try something more basic?' Cynthia suggests, bovine lips smooth and small beneath heavy-set horns.

Cynthia never writes anything down. Even if her hooves could grasp a pen, her notes would be useless in a month, or six months, or a year. I'm not a long-term patient. I don't need reassurances for the future. I don't carefully plot out reasons to continue to live while she supervises with sympathetic poise. She's given me paper to draw on, because I've made the mistake of expressing myself too often on a public canvas, and Kübler-Ross once said that a patient wants to be heard, even if they aren't speaking.

I craft a wobbly circle with a swift sweep of my hand. It's imperfect. It's unhappy.

'Like this?'

'You should draw what you know,' she amends.

I draw an angry 'V' in the middle of the circle. All I can hear is the stampeding of the animals, predators and prey, desperate to begin anew. Life roars within my head. I tell her, 'I know that Upper Palaeolithic mother goddess worship revolved around the idea of reincarnation, rebirth, and re-entry into the world.'

She hears my words, seizes on 'mother', and asks, 'Do you think that your death will upset your mother? And that by adhering to the belief of reincarnation, you can both find some peace?'

'I'm dying, not stupid.'

'It's normal to be afraid of dying.' Her voice is a mournful low. Her eyes are big and brown behind her glasses. I watch her lips form the words with great care. 'But you have to remember that it isn't your fault. You've done incredible things during your life.'

'I'm not afraid,' I say, because there's no point in being afraid of the inevitable anymore. 'And I haven't done anything incredible. And my mother never cries in public.'

'Why do you think that?'

'I don't think it. I know it.'

I trace over the 'V' again and again.

'The theory goes that it was an essential part of the natural cycle,' I say. Legs, mid-gallop. Upturned nostrils flare. Eyes flash with anticipation. 'Like rain. The spirits had to be released to replenish the herd.'

The bison tries to grant me closure. 'Maybe your fixation on the idea of a mother goddess is because you think that your mother wasn't enough.'

'My mother was more than enough. She even showed emotion once or twice.'

'And these animals, are they your family?'

Animals have leapt onto the page. Stick-legged and potbellied, they could have been drawn thousands of years ago on a cave wall: bears, hyenas, dogs, swans, snakes.

'They're my children,' I say.

'I see.'

Cynthia doesn't see. She still thinks I'm talking about my mother.

'I'm replenishing the herd,' I tell her. 'I'm releasing their spirits. I'm letting them go.'

'And the "V"?'

'Don't you understand?'

She doesn't, until I make a rude gesture, fingers jerking upwards between my legs.

Later, I scribble on the whiteboard with red until the

marker runs out of ink and then I press my hand into the ochre. I am eternal. I am part of the endless cycle of death and rebirth. I have passed through the trials and emerged victorious. I have left my mark.

The next day, my whiteboard is erased.

Day eleven. My youngest siblings spend the afternoon pretending to have a sleepover on my floor, grasping and pawing, snuffling from elongated snouts. With the curtains drawn, my room is a den and they're a hibernal memory, music played underwater, hot breath resonating beneath the covers until it becomes so stifling that I have to breach the surface to suck in the cold night air.

'How's school?' I ask. I am drowning.

'Good.' She's drawing, sitting cross-legged in the small space. I join her. Her lines are steadier than mine. I've been here forever and forever and the paint on the walls is peeling, peeling away. I draw and I draw and I draw. Occupational therapy, my cow-lipped therapist called it. One day soon, the paper will be gathered up and distributed like party favours from the dead.

They assure me that when I'm closer to dying, I'll go home to be more comfortable. I assure them I'm comfortable here. I don't want to be a burden on my family. They say I'm not a burden. I try to explain that my ghost would haunt my family's house if I died there, but I won't linger long here.

Around and around and around we go.

My brother shuffles in his sleeping bag. His iPad is propped up against his chest and the glare illuminates his face. I want to say, *Don't you know I could die at any moment, and then you'd be traumatised for life?*

Instead, because we're pretending it's a proper slumber party, I say to him, 'We're supposed to turn the overheads out soon.' I fold the piece of paper in half to cover a ladybug that struggles in a web. I start over, crumple the page, stare at the wall. 'But if you look sad enough, I bet they'll let us stay up later.'

'This is for you.' My sister passes me a drawing of a cat, yellow, with long whiskers.

I say, 'Thank you.'

'It's Cheddar,' she explains, 'our cat.'

'I know,' I lie. I draw Cheddar, our cat, from her reference.

'Why does he have six legs?'

'Because,' I say, picking up a green marker and drawing antennae on the head, 'it isn't really him. Cheddar is just fine. He'll be waiting for you when you get home.'

She takes the paper from me and begins to make additions: wings, a horn, a rainbow tail. She chews her lip. Each motion is deliberate. An artist at work.

I start a new drawing: a family, our family. My brother is snoring. I struggle with basic forms. They're meaningless blobs. I give them ears, eyes, whiskers, wings. Bears, a dog, a hyena, a swan. There're so many of them. I drop the marker twice. The headache that has been my constant is gone and I'm scared, suddenly, that I might close my eyes and not be able to open them.

My sister takes the drawing, critical. 'What's this?'

'Our family.'

Painstakingly, she helps me caption them with once familiar names. My brain is squeezed tight. It's just pressure. It doesn't hurt. *Any moment now*, it says, *any moment now*. It's growing heavy inside of me, choking, grasping, choking. The raft is sinking.

'I'm going to die,' I tell my sister. 'I'm going to die,' I tell my brother.

It's new all over again. A rediscovery of fear.

'I know.' She says it so earnestly that it can only be true. My brother mumbles a response. She's eight. He's ten. Fourteen and twelve years younger than me. They have, between them, more time than I ever will.

A valve opens, pressure releases. I catch my breath.

The nurse on duty – slithering and stealthy – stops by the room, cracks the door open, glances in at us. The sound is loud as thunder. We make eye contact. The overheads hum. My youngest brother is so engrossed in his video, he doesn't even notice. The serpent closes the door.

The lights stay on.

I wake up and seventeen days have passed since I moved in and everything is vibrant, everything is clear, everything makes sense. The respite stay has become permanent. I will die here, after all. The door opens. A golden retriever bounds in and covers me in kisses and then we walk in the garden, where topiary shades us from the worst of the heat.

'I miss you at home,' the dog barks.

'Why are you home?'

'Summer break.'

'Oh.'

There's a numbness. An exhaustion. If I stop moving, I won't be able to start again. I have a plastic cup full of ice that I can't swallow. I throw a ball and the dog fetches it for me, over and over. We sit by a fountain where the endless churning of water kicks up a fine mist. Salt settles on my lips like sea spray.

'I'm sorry,' I say. 'I can't remember your name.'

'Iris,' she says. I make the connection. My sister, this dog is my sister. A human. I try to see her. She's trying not to upset me and I'm trying not to get upset. She tells me, 'It's OK.'

The air is dry. I'm so transparent that the sunlight passes straight through me. The dog carries my cup of melting ice. She's fragile, so fragile. I say, 'I miss you.'

'I miss you, too.'

'It's movie night tonight. You should stay.'

'I'd like that,' she says. 'What're they watching?'

'Something awful, probably.'

'Bet you could find something worse.'

The movie starts before the sun sets, but we're the only ones watching, so I convince the nurse on duty to switch it to something funnier. My sister pre-empts every line and I laugh and she laughs and we eat little scoops of ice cream with plastic spoons out of disposable cups.

She looks at me once, when she thinks I'm watching the movie, and her eyes are round and watery and pleading, and I'm overwhelmed by the terrible feeling that I'm taking something from her that she will never get back.

'Since you're dying, Mom said I could have the pink sapphire.'

My elder sister sweeps into my room on the twentieth day, poised to strike. Her head swivels from side to side as she takes in my floral bedspread, my childish drawings, my empty plastic cups. Unblinking beady eyes fixate on me. She thinks she's being funny.

The ring in question already twinkles on her finger: simple, classic, tasteful. Metal and stone, more alive to her than I am. The pink sapphire is hers. She's victorious.

I am listless and hot, unable to get out of the padded chair I hauled in here two days ago. It takes up most of the space and makes my bed and desk seem tiny in comparison, but the red cushions are more comfortable, feel more important. I shift beneath the fleece blanket, turn away from the window.

I say, 'Congrats.'

Helen's face scrunches up, her perfect little nose crinkling. 'You look like shit.'

'I know.'

I don't, in fact, know. I don't want to see my reflection, shrivelling and withering into an insectoid that refuses to let go of life. My eyelashes, spider legs; my fingers, claws. My hair is a nest around my head, home to a hundred buzzing wasps, but there's no point in dragging a brush through the tangled mass and angering them further. Leave that to the mortician, the coroner, whoever the hell prepares bodies for death. It'll all be burned away anyways.

'How are you feeling?' Helen asks. She turns the ring over and over around her finger.

'I don't want to die,' I say. 'I like being alive.'

A spider has started to build her web in the top corner of my window. I refuse to let the facility manager take it down. I think that she's building it for me, this web, to catch my stray thoughts before they can flee. It arcs up, down, forms a shape that might be my face. It catches the light, this way and that, dust and dewdrops caught in sticky silk. Helen places her hand on my shoulder, sniffles. The cold ring digs into my paper-thin skin. I watch the spider spinning, spinning above me.

'I'm not dead yet,' I tell her. 'I'm still alive.'

My father calls, day after day, regardless of the hour. He leaves messages, short and to the point:
> *When are you free?*
> *Can I come see you?*
> *Call me. Call me. Call me.*

It keeps me awake, the phone lighting up and sending little squares of light creep-crawling across my desk, along the wall, to the ceiling. I listen to the messages on repeat.

> *I really miss you. Please, we should talk. I'd love to come see you. When are you available? Let me know. Love you.*

Longer, at night:

> *I was thinking about that time we went to the pumpkin patch, together, when you were little. Your mother and I used to say as long as you could pick the pumpkin up, you could keep it, and you did this thing – you were always like this – you'd find the biggest pumpkin you could and pick it up, somehow, and waddle across the field a few steps, and then we'd have to fit it in the trunk of the car to bring it home. And I don't know why I'm thinking about that. I'm just thinking of you.*

A picture of me accompanies the message, it must be me, wearing blue-and-white stripes, curled around a massive pumpkin. I'm smiling, or grimacing, and there are scuff marks in the dirt where I took shuffling steps to prove that yes, I could bear the weight.

The phone shimmies across the desk when I leave the ringer on, and then does the same when I turn the ringer off but can't figure out how to turn off vibrate. I want to destroy it, the phone, but I can't do that, either, because I'm too exhausted by the messages that he leaves me all the time.

I'm sorry, he says during the day, when the synthetic light barely bothers me. *I should've been there more.*

The phone is quiet for a few blissful hours, and then three words, the three words he's said and said and said but never meant:

I love you.

The days are all the same.

My oldest brother meets me at The Facility – always a capital 'T', for time, always a capital 'F', for finality – and he hands me a gift-wrapped package. His hyena-dappled skin and wide smile and laughing eyes are my anchor. Today, the seas are calm.

'I thought it'd be nice, you know, to keep up our weekly calls,' he explains. I tear off the wrapping paper covered in skulls and crossbones. It's a Ouija board, the box still sealed in a fine plastic film. When I shake it, it rattles.

'You shouldn't have.'

'Mom told me you wanted one, and I aim to please.'

We laugh. The building exhales and I pull a worn blanket around my shoulders. Bare-armed in the July heat, he pretends not to see.

I say, 'Tell me something good.'

'I'm going to school in the fall, despite my best efforts.'

'Having a degree is important,' I say. Mine's propped up in the corner of my room by an illicit and unlit scented candle, the faux-leather case embossed with my full name. Soon, I'll be a college-educated corpse.

'A learned woman.' He nods sagely.

'I truly am an inspiration to us all.'

The common room has been wallpapered since I was last here. A frog gives a wide-mouthed grin from a dew-laden leaf. A monkey swings from vine to vine. A tiger peers out from behind a tree stump. A spider dangles from a fine silken line.

'What's the prognosis?'

'Any day now, they say.'

'They've been saying that forever.'

He wants to drag life out of me. The days stretch on and on and on for him. But for me, the pressure behind my eyes has given way to a cold numbness, and the pain is gone, and it all feels simple.

'I think this is really it.'

'Yeah?'

'Yeah.'

'It was nice knowing you, then.'

'Likewise.'

He's snuck in a lighter. We sit together on the floor, the Ouija board between us, and hold a séance with a candle that smells of sandalwood and jasmine. The heart-shaped token glides beneath our fingers.

Hello, hello, hello.

We ask, 'How old were you?'

We ask, 'How did you die?'

We ask, 'Who did you love?'
Goodbye, goodbye, goodbye.

Un

Louie Conway

The young man leans on the granite counter in the northwest corner of the newly renovated kitchen-living area of his sister's home. The screen of his smartphone is eight inches from his eyes, a dark reflector amid the beams of bright sunlight entering through transom windows set in three of the room's four walls. Nestled in the folds of his right ear is a wireless earphone, playing at low volume a podcast interview with a controversial public intellectual whose work applies Darwinian principles to a range of social, professional and romantic problems (mainly those commonly encountered by males in the young man's age cohort), an interview which the young man has heard many times before and which therefore currently exerts only a weak and sporadic grip on his attention. A faint smile lingers on his face, the remnant of a laugh provoked by a surreal joke about the logic of werewolves he read seven seconds ago, further up the social media feed he is scrolling through with his right thumb. The smile has now faded almost completely as his attention alights on phone-camera footage of a rocket strike on a tank in a war happening somewhere hilly and arid. The projectile, a quivering white-hot orb, enters the frame from bottom right and shrinks off towards the tank in the left background; the orb vanishes, then the tank explodes, its khaki steel turret replaced by a swirling nova of red flame and black smoke, killing everyone inside. The young man watches the silent twelve-second video impassively and scrolls on.

Currently hidden from the young man's view by the large kitchen island is the eleven-month-old niece he has been tasked with watching while his sister drives the short distance into town for formula. With increasing confidence and speed the baby crawls along the base of the room's east wall, her small hands slapping the cool, varnished-stone tiles chosen by her parents from a catalogue three months ago, her soft knees shuffling forward and her dainty, downy head, still spongy in sections where the bones are yet to fuse, lurching from side to side – movements which appear comically ungoverned but are in fact the product of intense concentration, the baby only having learned to crawl unassisted less than a week ago.

Objects located within the baby's foot-high plane of access include: four square metres of interlocking foam tiles; two paperboard children's books; a scattered set of brightly coloured building blocks; a fine shard of glass, missed during the clean-up after her father dropped a champagne flute while toasting the renovation; the hardwood legs of a dining table and four chairs; the cat's bed (empty); the cat, rubbing its flank along the room's west wall with its head turned to eye the baby through the chair legs; a sky-blue woollen cap, shaken from the baby at the outset of her crawl and lying in the shadow of the kitchen island; eighteen metres of timber skirting board, installed in a distracted hurry by a local tradesman following a phone call informing him his mother-in-law had suffered another fall; three nail heads, protruding slightly from the skirting board along the base of the east wall; a week-old morsel of roast chicken, dropped during the serving of last Sunday's roast dinner – which now catches the baby's attention and reorients the angle of her crawl – containing traces of Campylobacter and E. coli; two common garden spiders; one cardinal spider; one daddy longlegs; a safety pin (closed); a five-cent coin; the young man's socked feet and bare calves.

In the moments between his closing one social media app and opening another, the young man becomes aware of assorted slaps and gurgles of exertion coming from somewhere on the other side of the kitchen and remembers with a quick-passing volt of anxiety that a baby has been left in his care. Almost coincident with this feeling arrives the sound of a resonant ping from the young man's phone, its screen now aglow with a message from the young woman on his university course who, despite not having heard from her since the end of term, he has thought about at least once every waking hour of every day of the summer break. The sound of the ping and the sight of her name and profile picture (in which she's wearing a light summer dress and playfully yet gracefully straddling a small statue of a dolphin in some sunny seaside locale) triggers a release of dopamine sufficient to instantly improve his mood, causing him to reinterpret the sounds coming from the other side of the kitchen as indications that the baby is contented and safe and not in need of his immediate attention.

The message contains a link to a song which the young woman mentioned during a conversation that the young man thought ended badly, due to his confidently espousing a set of values regarding the role of the male in a monogamous heterosexual relationship. After the young woman's heartfelt description of the song (titled 'Househusband') which the young man admitted to never having heard, he had segued awkwardly into a monologue about how the male's optimal role in modern relationships is essentially that of the hunter in tribal societies ten millennia ago, a role which finds contemporary expression in the form of the male working to earn money with which to buy food and maintain shelter for the female while she cares for their offspring, values which the young man is not even sure he holds or entirely understands, but merely read (in the controversial public intellectual's book) that women find attractive due to a biological hardwiring that compels them to select mates in accordance with a set of normatively masculine criteria – strength, height, status, ambition, practical competence, etc. – whether they're aware of it or not.

The young man inferred from the young woman's reaction to his monologue that she was put off, even slightly offended, by it, by him. But now her message prompts him to consider the possibility that his attempts to inflate his appeal as a potential mate may have had the intended effect. Lying one level below this thought is a competing theory (to which the young man is inclined to ascribe less credence) which posits that the young woman might just like him for who he is; for his unashamedly nerdy sense of humour and tendency to laugh generously at other people's jokes; for his sharp, unusually high-bridged nose; for the way he quietly clears his throat and squints before answering a question. As these theories jostle for supremacy in his mind, the young man realises he is unsure which of them he would prefer to be true. If her attraction to him (if indeed she is attracted to him) is a result of things he has done and said with the express purpose of making her attracted to him, this would suggest he has a measure of influence over the feelings of others, and can therefore alter them to his benefit by acting the right way and saying the right things. On the other hand, if she has come to like him merely for who he is, this would be due to factors outside his control – namely her own independent thoughts and feelings – and that this state of affairs did not arise directly from his intentions suggests he has little say in whether or not in the future it suddenly changes.

Though the young man is not aware of it, his inclination to doubt the latter theory issues from a region of his subconscious that contains a primitive model of his relationship with his own mother, who, while she showed an almost overbearing affection for the young man for most of his childhood, was given to sudden, often weeks-long periods of emotional coldness towards him, characterised by outbursts of rage at the smallest transgressions and comments that undermined any positive thing he did. Since the young man could never identify what he might have done to provoke any of his mother's cold periods, he concluded that he had little influence over how his relationships with others played out, causing every close relationship he has formed since to be attended by ambient levels of paranoia and dread.

Deciding finally that the theory which provides him with the greater sense of comfort is probably true, the young man replies to the young woman's message with several flame emojis, a response of general enthusiasm obviating the need to express verbally anything specific about the song, since he has not listened to it yet and does not intend to any time soon, the artist being one he merely faked interest in when speaking with the young woman in order to appear informed and of similar taste; after which he types and sends the message: *got it on loud while I look after my baby niece*, hoping this will put an image in the young woman's mind of the young man as capable of caring for infants, further hoping that this image taps some primordial well of unconscious yearning within the young woman to bear and care for children, a yearning she might henceforth associate with the young man and misinterpret, in the near term, as a desire to have sex with him.

Two ticks appear beside each of the young man's messages to indicate that the young woman has both received and read them, a few seconds after which her status bar at the top of the messaging app switches to *Offline*. The young man immediately becomes anxious that the young woman has detected his latest attempt to control her perception of him, a worry which manifests physically as a plummeting sensation at his centre and a bristling heat on his cheeks. The modest cocktail of adrenaline and cortisol released into his bloodstream sharpens his senses, causing him to perform a brisk scan of the environment for immediate dangers. This is when he looks down to his left and sees his niece, emerging head first from behind the kitchen island and crawling at a steady pace towards the fridge, just as the sunlight, entering through the window at the young man's back to spread itself in a clean rhombus on the tiles as if to light the way, catches some jagged scrap of reflective matter lying like a trap in the baby's path, awaiting the fall of her small, soft hand and glaring, as the young man's instinctive lunge towards the baby alters his sightline, suddenly brighter, forcing his eyes to reflexively close even as he continues to move at speed across the kitchen, throwing his left foot out before him in a blind lunging stride and landing it on the baby's wool cap, the foot then slipping cartoonishly up and away from the floor as the dual action of gravity and momentum causes the young man's body to become momentarily airborne, flailing through its silent apex before plunging floorwards and pulling the trailing weight of his head down on the kitchen counter, whose sharp granite corner connects powerfully with the left temporal region of the young man's skull before sending it on its way, hard and fast and heavy, towards the cool varnished-stone tiles of the kitchen floor.

Having sensed a commotion to her left, stopped dead in her crawl and turned her head towards the sound of a biting *crack*, the baby takes in the scene of the young man splayed on the tiles with his eyes shut and mouth ajar as when pretending for her amusement to be asleep, and waits to see what will happen next. But before the rising hunch that *something is wrong* has even reached the baby's mind, the living, breathing field of tessellating polychromatic patterns and reverberant sounds through which she perceives the world has begun to transform. Only seconds ago, the sun's rays were warm, guiding presences that seemed to radiate from the very surfaces that reflected them, columns of kind energy generated by swirling interactions between elements in the stone tiles' washed pattern, which itself rippled like clear shallow shorewater at the baby's touch. The young man's laugh and the mewlings of the cat were visible things, travelling in soft sonar-like wavelets of reassurance through the medium of the air and trailing – like all things the baby perceives – tapering fractal mosaics of colour; the baby's brain being, at this early stage of development, comparable to the brain of an adult under the influence of hallucinogenic drugs: wide open and hypersensitive, the fluid signal-sharing between its budding components and interlacing networks producing a synaesthetic tapestry of all sensory phenomena, the intensity, theme and colour palette of which are determined by the emotional state of the baby, and the emotional states of others as perceived by the baby – the crucial difference being that her experience is untainted by knowledge of what a hallucination even *is*, or of the personal and social expectations that contaminate such experiences when induced pharmacologically in adults, freeing the baby from worries about whether she is acting strangely or making others uncomfortable, whether she consumed too much of a certain compound or not enough, whether the effects she feels will be felt forever or are already wearing off, a freedom that permits a feeling of constant, pure, self-sustaining awe, unexpecting and unself-conscious, the significance in all things issuing not from some profundity-seeking impulse within the experiencer, but emanating from *the things themselves*.

But now as the feeling that *something is wrong* overwhelms the baby's attention, the sun's rays, as if in sympathy, run cold over the tiles, and the shadows cast by them solidify and deepen and grotesquely contort, and the fizzing pinks and greens that trailed every moving thing are reduced to slicks of blue-black effluent that run like oil over the kitchen counters and creep like tentacles down their sides. And at the centre of the baby's teeming, shrinking field of vision lies the young man's body, so starkly divested of the radiant animating force the baby has, since their very first meeting, so adored about the young man, that aura of exuberant mischief and spry, unseasoned intelligence which seems to bring the baby's mother, whenever the young man comes home from wherever he has been, such profound happiness – tears of laughter as they catch up over cups of steaming tea, smiles of deep joy as she watches the young man read the baby a story – an aura which itself surrounds, protectively, something the baby sees glowing at the heart of every living thing: a small but immovable core of pure, bright loving-kindness, which, in the young man's case, is subtly flecked and swirled, like some beautifully flawed marble, by self-doubt, and fear of the future, and the need to feel loved in return.

Sh. Shh. Sean. Uncle Sean. Sean: a sound like water rushing from the tap at bath time, like the shushing of the mother as she lowers the baby into her cot, like the white noise left playing in the room as the baby twitches on the edge of sleep; a comforting sound, which has followed the young man like a super-aura around his aura ever since the mother began to point at him and intone, 'Uncle *Sean*. That's your Uncle *Sean*. Say "*Hi Uncle Sean!*"'; pointing then at other things and people ('and that's *Mummy*, and *Daddy*, and *Grandma*, and *pussycat*, and *ball* . . .'), before always lastly pointing at the baby herself ('and . . . Lily! Hi, *Lily*. We *love* you, *Lily*.'), a ritual through which the baby has come to understand the world as reducible into categories, an indefinitely vast space populated by discrete objects with dedicated names and stable locations, the ritual's final step ('That's *right*. That's *you*. You're *Lily*!') serving to gradually instil the baby with a sense of self and identity, of being discontinuous with the world, of having an ego, of being an 'I' that is located (as far as the baby can tell from where her mother is pointing) somewhere behind the baby's eyes – an illusion, but one through which all experience will henceforth be mediated.

So strong is her association between the sound 'Uncle Sean' and the young man's animating force that the baby believes if she could only utter the sound then it would ripple through the air's medium and enter the young man's body, instantly *reinspiriting* him, a line of reasoning which to adult minds seems unfathomably naive but in fact suggests an understanding of the causal power of language and the relationship between stimulus and response that is advanced for the baby's age. But lagging behind her slight intellectual precocity is the development of the baby's facial muscles, which are still too weak to form the shapes required to mimic sounds and words, and indeed it is this gulf between her capacities for understanding and expression that accounts for why she sometimes cries apropos of apparently nothing, for these are the frustrated wails of an increasingly intelligent mind trapped in a weak, recalcitrant body. And now as she watches dumbly on, a trickle of blood – like the sinister twin of the smiling worm that peeks out from an apple in her favourite picture book – emerges from the young man's left ear and runs abruptly down his neck, marking his whitening skin with a bright-red line, the tip of which wriggles slightly on its journey floorwards as if itself alive and intent upon the coolness of the tiles. Tears well on the verges of the baby's eyelids. Though it will be years before she grasps the concepts 'alive' and 'dead' and the distinction between them, the baby understands with a kind of instinctive visceral despair that a process of change is underway which, once complete, cannot be reversed. The baby wants it to stop, wants the young man to wake up with a sudden laugh like he does when pretending to be asleep, but now as she strains painfully the muscles of her tear-streaked face in an attempt to speak her uncle's name she produces only a sputter of meaningless syllables – 'Ssssuu. Un. Uuun . . .' – her lips fumbling uselessly around the word the way her cold hands, on winter mornings several years from now, will fumble around a zip.

Meanwhile shattered pieces of the young man's skull, having punctured the outermost two of the three protective meninges surrounding his brain on impact with the counter, continue to exert pressure on the innermost meninge, pressing it hard against the tender, gelatinous mass of the young man's temporal lobe, the resultant strain on surrounding capillaries having just seconds ago caused several hundred thousand of them to burst virtually in unison. Blood building in the subarachnoid crevice has overflowed into the auditory canal and begun to trickle out of the young man's ear.

Though the sheer force of his head's contrecoup impact with the granite counter caused a sudden and near-total cessation of subjective experience – his consciousness reduced to an insensate, identityless hum much like that of a patient's under general anaesthetic – electrochemical activity in the young man's brain has since resumed beyond the level sufficient for a minimally conscious state, a kind of paralysed stupor in which his centreless attention is snagged and released by a sequence of dreamlike vignettes arising from the subconscious flux of formative memories, deep fears, cherished hopes, hidden desires . . . It's a busy Tuesday night in the student union, and he is approaching a woman standing alone beside the bar. He feels a murky sort of attraction to her, akin to homely warmth aswirl on an eddy of shame. But due to damage now spreading through regions of his brain responsible for long-term memory and facial recall – the trauma surrounding the site of the skull fracture expanding out across the temporal lobe and in towards the hippocampus as the many axons severed by the jarring of skull against brain degenerate and release toxic neurotransmitters into extracellular space – the young man does not recognise her. The woman is his mother. She begins speaking in a language that, though it has the cadences and phonetic profile of English, the young man does not understand, a result of the damage having now reached those areas in his brain's posterior related to language comprehension, though not, as yet, those in the anterior related to speech, allowing him, in the vignette, to say, 'Do I know you from somewhere?' – precisely the sort of opening line the controversial public intellectual would recommend a male use in situations where he should reasonably be expected to know the attractive female he's addressing it to (having met her several times before, say), the question subliminally communicating that the female is not all that memorable, or at least not all that memorable to the male, who, evidently, meets more attractive women than he can care to remember, this fact indicating a high level of social status which the female will (the controversial public intellectual claims) find attractive, her attraction (in theory) compounded by insecurities about whether she herself is attractive or memorable at all. The woman reacts badly, sharpening the tone of her nonsense speech, raising her voice. The young man, having so far felt uncomfortably warm in the sweaty air of the busy student union, whose crowd tonight, he now realises, comprises every dead and living person he's ever known (a fact which he merely *feels* to be true since he is unable to recognise a single one of their faces), registers a thick, tremulous chill travelling from the tips of his toenails to the ends of the hairs on his head as the dramatic fluctuations in body temperature caused by ongoing severe blood loss are integrated into the vignette. There is a pressure in his left ear like the feeling of trapped pool water; the young man looks into the mirror behind the bar and sees a man he half-recognises with blood pouring down his neck in a jagged stream. A figure moves in front of the image; his sister – though he knows her only to the extent that he feels a sudden calm in her presence, the lack of a need to say or do anything that might improve her feelings towards him since they are both immune to manipulation and unconditionally positive – is standing behind the bar, regarding him with kind eyes and a head slightly cocked as if to say, 'I'll love you whoever you are – but *who are you?*' But now when her mouth opens to speak it produces only a sputter of meaningless syllables –

'Uun. Sss. Unnn.' – her voice seeming to emanate from the student union's sound system, high-pitched as an infant's.

This is when the young man registers a subtle change in the room's atmosphere; every person in the crowd, as if sharing one mind, seems to become aware of his presence. They do not speak to him or stare but continue with their drinking and talking and dancing, all the while stealing glances at him so deft he could be imagining them; snippets of conversation that reach him contain whispers of his name. They mean him well (he understands this), but they are waiting for him to act. He looks to the older woman beside him, then to the younger woman behind the bar for clues as to what he should do. The women are crying quietly, each with one arm raised, pointing at something. He follows their fingers, sees the neon sign above a fire door on the far side of the dance floor reading 'EXIT'; another chill engulfs him as he moves towards it, one so deep this time it shakes his bones.

Here the vignette abruptly ends. Awash in his blood but deprived of its glucose-and-oxygen payload for almost four minutes now, the young man's brain is no longer capable of projecting three-dimensional spaces and populating them with people, is no longer – as the energy encoding the subconscious flux breaks free of defunct underpinning networks and dissipates into surrounding dead tissue – able to dream or remember or hallucinate, to process sensory pleasure or physical pain, to focus his attention or order his thoughts, to sustain the illusion, ingrained since infancy, that he is a single, unified self with fears and needs and desires all his own, separate from the world and from others, a lonely universe unto himself. His brain is dying, and with it goes all memory of his family: the way his mother laughed and smelled and attempted to reason verbally with the cat, the way she dabbed her eyes with a bent wrist when they wept over diced onions, or at the string-swept finales of sentimental films, or in the act of being unaccountably cold towards the young man, as though the coldness was something she couldn't help, that she did in spite of herself, a deeper, truer, kinder self that was trapped mutely inside her and couldn't bear to see him hurt. So too go the many different selves the young man inhabited in the company of particular people: the effortless comedian he was in the company of his sister, the slightly insecure and excitable child he regressed to around friends, the outwardly pompous but inwardly frightened confusion of hormones he became in the company of the young woman and the restless, self-reproachful, fruitlessly ruminative young man who agonised when alone over which of these selves, if any, was the *real him*.

But there is Something left. Something which now, as the final flickers of electricity in the young man's brain go dark, removes Itself from this corner of the physical world, or, rather, removes this corner of the physical world from Itself, as if the young man all along was merely one of many headsets It wore in order to explore finite tracts on the infinite landscape of possible experiences, to explore *Itself*, through interactions with other living beings which, from the cat to the baby to the three men between the ages of nineteen and twenty-eight who died in the exploding tank, are, or were, all just other temporary manifestations of It. And though this egress or disentanglement from the physical causes It to become briefly identical with profound suffering, it also entails, as the suffering ebbs away, increasing clarity and intensity of those qualities like love, mercy, meaning and togetherness which both derive from and ultimately define It, and which can be accessed or embodied by the physical world only in their severely diminished, imperfect forms – and yet:

now,

and *now*,

and *now*,

eyes elsewhere are opening with the light of It behind them shining out.

The baby has been frozen in place on her hands and knees staring through the tear-blurred portals of her eyes at the young man's lifeless body for almost four minutes when she hears the thundery crunch of her mother's car's tyres on the gravel surrounding the house and for the first time reacts to this sound not with joyous excitement at her mother's imminent appearance but with a wave of impotent, anticipatory sorrow, born of the baby's inarticulable, inscrutable-even-to-herself intuition that the contours of this situation are about to expand and engulf the happiness of another person she loves.

Which now they do, the baby's mother having entered the front door, hung her keys on the hook in the hallway, walked through to the kitchen-living area and frozen on its threshold at the sight of her brother sprawled on the tiles with a rapidly widening circle of blood around his head, causing the baby's mother to loose a scream of such blistering pitch and volume that it induces in the baby a 'flight' response sufficiently acute to send her body into metabolic chaos, forcing her brain, in order that her vital rhythms and involuntary cycles continue functioning, to enforce a kind of emergency neural quarantine around the parts of itself that hold a record of the scream – that hold a record of the entire experience.

And because the countless random subatomic perturbations of energy that will ultimately determine the future's course have not yet occurred, it is not fated what exactly will cause these memories – these quiescent neural clusters sealed off behind makeshift neural structures – to detonate inside what will be, by then, a grown woman's brain: the sight of blood wriggling worm-like from the nose of an overdosing lover; the bony pop of a wind-filled bin liner tacked on a broken window; sawdust particles adrift on a refurbished psychiatric ward – or nothing external at all, just the slow inevitable overload caused by carrying unprocessed memories of death within the strained and fraying network of the self. But detonate they eventually will, spreading as flares of charged chemicals through node and network and hemisphere, shocking every cortical layer and lobe so that when in that moment of cold, bewildering recognition the woman opens her mouth to speak, she will produce only a sputter of meaningless syllables.

Sss. Un . . . Un.

The Birth of a Devil Sheep

David McGrath

Willy Byrne's fuck-your-mother swagger was a swagger to mug you off, a swagger to warn, were half a chance given, he would *actually* fuck your mother, a deed he had done to many a man of Ballybalt. Maura Byrne had breastfed him to fourteen then to eighteen she beat him with the brush until she drowned herself in the Slay River, irreparably crossing every single wire in the man's head. He had been quoted as saying he couldn't do it with a woman who *wasn't* a mother – not unless, he said, he equipped himself with two lollipop sticks and an elastic band.

Unsurprisingly, full-time employment was somewhat of a hindrance. Willy Byrne had been thrown off more building sites than asbestos for his inclination towards the maternal. For pint-money, he odd-jobbed for town-folk with no mothers above ground. The Crack, having assumed his own elderly mother safe from the clutches of the infamous motherfucker, had Willy Byrne up to the farm to do some painting and weed the garden. Down in Phelan's, with a few too many pints on board, The Crack had supposedly said he may as well have hired Stevie Wonder for all the spilled paint and missed weeds. The words were sucked in and belched about the snug of Phelan's for days on gossip-hound breath until they eventually rested on the ears of Willy Byrne himself.

'Little dwarf bastard,' Willy Byrne said. 'I'll show him a Stevie fuckin' Wonder.'

And the gossip-hounds sat back and sipped their pints with smiles on, because this was Ballybalt, a town of lunatics, bullshit-artists and story-mongers, always a spit from self-annihilation, fashioning their normalcy against distorted, twisted and embellished stories of everyone else's abnormality. Stories were the entertainment.

At a certain age that varied from man to man, when futility was recognised, the men of Ballybalt would resign themselves to Tom Phelan's snug to see who could hang there the longest, collecting stories like scalps. Tom Phelan would nail the fallen's photographs to the wall for reminder, fallen men like Seanie Pender who when the bank came to repossess, knocked his house down with his JCB then paid the bank a visit to blow out its windows with his shotgun. A year later he was elected to Dáil Éireann. Two years after that he was found dead in suspicious circumstances in a Dublin brothel. The men in Phelan's drank over the Seanie Pender story, nodding creamy pints of stout at him and the rest of the dead and buried men on the wall, using their stories as both inspiration and warning depending on the conversation. When a photograph went up, the story of it belonged to everybody, to do with as they saw fit, adding details to details, forming the story to make sense of the senseless, sometimes tangling the original story so much in fabrication that it became an out-of-control juggernaut of a story that had to be reined back in by the realists.

Not long after the Stevie Wonder comment, The Crack got up like any other day to tend his sheep, only to find Willy Byrne in his kitchen eating a bowl of cornflakes. Willy Byrne was wearing just his underpants, his balls sagging out the left leg of them. All The Crack could do was stand there, his mouth agape, knowing what had gone on but wishing to Baby Jesus it had not, too stunned to take a toaster to Willy Byrne's head, too stunned to even say anything. Willy Byrne slurped the last bit of milk from the bowl then said, 'That aul one of yours could suck a frozen turkey through a tennis racket, Crack. Right, I may go up and get me trousers.'

The gossip-hounds rallied in pseudo-condemnation of Willy Byrne's latest triumph. 'That was terrible, Byrne. A new low for you this is,' they said down in Phelan's. 'The Crack's mother is nearly eighty years old with an onset of Alzheimer's.'

'Didn't hear her complaining,' said Willy Byrne back to them.

'You're an awful man.'

'How in the name of God does he be at it with all these mothers in anyways?'

'He does tell them he only has six weeks to live and all sorts.'

'There's a mini-mam,' said Willy Byrne, 'but I never heard tell of a maxi-mam.'

'Awful man altogether. Doesn't The Crack have enough to be worrying about with Satanists up there hassling him about his geep?'

'The Satanists came after,' Willy Byrne said. 'I

wouldn't have done it had I known he had Satanists up there. I'm bad but I'm not that bad.'

Satanists had arrived on the perimeter of The Crack's farm after the unlikely union of sheep and goat that resulted in the birth of a goat-sheep or geep, as they were known. Usually a geep was stillborn, but not this geep whose goat father was a dog-tormentor and as brazen as he was tough. Furthermore, the ewe in question was always getting her head caught in the fence trying for faraway hills, so between the pair of them, any offspring would be determined.

The geep had sparked national interest because it was August, silly season, and feck-all else was going on in the world. A photographer and journalist came down to Ballybalt. The Crack's big, round and red, camera-freaked head was in the *Farmers Journal* the next week holding the geep on his little lap. A dwarf sheep farmer holding a geep. They put it on the front page. This was how a group of Satanists got wind of it. What Satanists were doing reading the *Farmers Journal*, nobody knew. So then, as though the man didn't have enough to contend with, The Crack had sheep to shear, a sick mother to care for, and a gaggle of Satanists chanting at all hours of the morning about the coming of Lucifer. To top it off, the goat was walking around the yard with a Willy Byrne swagger, more confidence than ever to upset his dog. He was half-thinking to shoot the bastarding goat. It would at least appease the dog's problems and ensure no more births of goat-sheep to entice even more Satanists down from whereverthefuck.

'A total buncha cunts youse are,' The Crack shouted at them from a safe distance, his tractor ticking over, and his foot to the clutch, ready to escape if they went berserk on being called cunts.

'All we ask for is updates on the geep, Mr Crack, whether it makes marks in the ground or has any unusual rituals,' the head Satanist shouted back.

'Would yis ever cop on, lads. I've enough to be getting on with than having to deal with this shite.'

'As we said before, Mr Crack, we're very much willing to purchase the geep from you and be on our way.'

'And what would you intend to do with the geep?'

'Sacrifice it.'

'Ah would you all ever fuck off to fuck.'

It was time to give Father Horsebox a ring.

Father Horsebox was so called because as a young priest, he was caught stomping out the back of Tom Phelan's horsebox while fastening his belt, followed two seconds later by his dishevelled housekeeper, a look of sweaty sex on both their faces, and it became quite clear what had been going on.

'They done it in me horsebox,' Tom Phelan town-cried.

'Go 'way out of that, Tom,' the town cried back.

'No word of a lie, lads. Doing up his belt he was, and the look of sweaty sex on their faces was unmistakable.'

'Why would they be doing it in *your* horsebox, Tom, eh?'

'Sure, wasn't he looking to buy it.'

'Jaysus,' went the town. 'In the horsebox?'

'In me fuckin' horsebox!'

'He does come alive in an equine atmosphere,' said the philosophers.

'Aye, the fuckin' bookies,' said the realists.

Gambling was Father Horsebox's vice, as was drinking whiskey, swearing, smoking and women. He was also prone to occasional acts of vandalism and larceny when the gambling, drinking and women were not going so well. On the face of it, Father Horsebox was a terrible priest who, truth be told, didn't believe in God and should have been excommunicated in his first week out of the seminary. The thing was, Father Horsebox was Rambo in a crisis and that, in a nutshell, was what Jesus was all about.

Father Horsebox was probably bigger and better than Jesus in anyways. For starters, he had a phone number. Secondly, he was an artist in talking down a nervous breakdown. Jesus was all about not doing it in the first place whereas Father Horsebox was all about dealing with it when it was done. The fallen men who were hung on the wall of Phelan's would have fell a lot sooner had it not been for Father Horsebox.

But times were changing, as they always changed, and gone were the days when a nervous breakdown was simply bundled into the back seat of the car then held there by his two brothers all the way to St John of Gods. It had to be free will now – they had to go to alcohol rehabilitation, or wherever, of their own accord which was a growing pain in Father Horsebox's bollocks.

'Mother of Christ on it anyway,' said Father Horsebox, lifting his mouth out from between the housekeeper's legs. 'Hello?'

'Father, it's Dallas Dunne here. Me dad's locked himself in his room and he won't come out. Is there any chance you could come over and talk to him?'

'I'll be over shortly, Dallas. Put the kettle on for a hot

whiskey for me, would you, darling?'

'Grand.'

'Grand, then,' said Father Horsebox, hung up and cut the foreplay short. 'Sorry, Eileen, I've to be quick about it. Brendan Dunne's barricaded himself in his bedroom,' he said, pulling his underpants down and mounting her.

Brendan Dunne's young lad was smoking hash outside the house as Father Horsebox rolled up in his Micra.

'He says he's throwing you down the stairs if you go up, Horsebox,' the young lad said.

'It's Father Horsebox to you, you little prick. Has Dallas a whiskey ready for me?'

'I dunno t'fuck.'

'What's going on with your father?'

'Locked himself in his room and won't come out.'

'Well I know that much.'

'We've no dog, Horsebox – so you have your work cut out for you.'

'No dog?'

'Nope.'

'Curse of fuckin' God on it anyway.'

'May think of something else for your big finale.'

'Fuck off, you little bollocks.'

'No way. I'm hanging around here to watch you getting thrown down our stairs.'

There was one thing Father Horsebox relied on when talking down a nervous breakdown – a family dog. Without one, he was in unknown territory and the hash-smoking little bollocks of a young lad sitting on the wall knew it.

*

The Crack had called the parochial house but Father Horsebox was out. The housekeeper asked him to leave a message.

'Well, do you have a pen?' he asked.

'I do,' she said but The Crack knew full well that the housekeeper was a doddery aul one that wouldn't know the difference between a pen and a Tuesday.

'Just tell him it's getting bad with these Satanists, would you, Eileen?'

'Satanists,' she repeated. 'Getting sad.'

'*Bad*,' The Crack said. 'It's getting *bad* with these Satanists.'

'How bad, Crack?'

'Is there a scale for how bad it gets with Satanists? Grand so, tell him it's a nine on how bad it gets with Satanists, would you, Eileen?'

'A nine?' she repeated. 'That bad?'

'Well, I'm keeping my goat-sheep inside in the house for fear of kidnap even though it's scaring the bejesus out of me because it has acquired a taste for chicken and won't eat anything else. And never in a million years did I think I'd say this but I've brought the ewe inside too because Willy Byrne has got wind of the situation and I think he wants to have intercourse with her because it's mother to Satan incarnate. He's lurking about outside with the gaggle of Satanists who are chanting about it being very close to the second blood supermoon. It's getting pretty bad, you know?'

'That does sound like a nine, all right. But, you may tell him yourself because I won't remember all that.'

'What's his fuckin' number?'

*

The stairs were put in retrospectively when the Dunnes converted the attic. Having had limited space for them, the architect was forced to give them an incline more vertical than a usual staircase. A fall down them would have been detrimental to one's spine and hip, two bones that were not in great shape anyway due to Eileen's increasingly voracious sexual appetite.

'Dallas, darling,' Father Horsebox said, 'put an aul mattress halfway up the stairs there, would you, love?'

'He won't throw you down them, Father,' Dallas said.

'Twenty quid says he will,' the young lad said.

'Shut up to fuck,' Dallas told him then apologised to Father Horsebox for swearing.

'Brendan! I'm coming up. I would greatly appreciate it if you weren't to throw me down the stairs when I go up there.'

The lack of response came threatening down the stairs as fast as a falling priest. It excited the stoned young lad who held his phone up and pressed Record. 'I am going to make a fortune out of this.'

'Brendan, it would be great if you didn't throw me down the stairs that's all I'm saying. Your young lad seems to think it inevitable. I'd really like it if you proved him wrong.'

'He's telling you what to do in your own house, Brendan,' the young lad shouted.

Dallas clipped him on the ear.

'Right, I'm coming up,' Father Horsebox shouted.

Father Horsebox, being a representative of existence, had to come to its defence quite often, particularly at barricaded bedroom doors. He had knocked on worse but the bedroom door of an incensed widower seeking revenge on existence was still a tough day's work.

'Brendan,' he began, 'if it was the other way around, Brendan, and it was Sharon locked up inside the bedroom and heartbroken. What I mean to say is, you're alive for her now, Brendan, so that she doesn't have to bear the weight of such sadness.'

'Fuck off, Horsebox,' Brendan Dunne said.

Father Horsebox's phone rang. 'Oh curse of fuck on it in anyways,' he said when he saw it was The Crack doing the calling. 'Howaya, Crack. Satanists, Crack? Am I hearing you correctly? And you haven't had a drop to drink? Willy Byrne is what? Chanting what exactly? Right well, I'll be out as soon as I can, Crack.'

Father Horsebox hung up the phone. 'And I thought I heard it all.'

'What was that about?' Brendan Dunne asked.

Bingo, thought Father Horsebox. Without a dog, a geep being tormented by Satanists was the next best thing.

'Satanists are on The Crack's farm after his geep,' Father Horsebox said. 'They think it's the coming of Lucifer and I think Willy Byrne wants to ride it.'

'That fuckin' Willy Byrne.'

'That fuckin' Willy Byrne is right, Brendan. He's an awful man altogether. And that poor little geep, Brendan – didn't have a great start to begin with, what with not being accepted as either a sheep or a goat, and now it's all scared and worried – never done nothing to nobody and them bloody Satanists want to sacrifice it to Lucifer, what?'

There was a silence.

Father Horsebox put his finger to his lips to tell

Dallas and the young lad to shut the fuck up and allow the innocence of animals to resonate.

The key turned in the bedroom door.

'Here we go,' the young lad said.

Brendan Dunne came out, red-eyed and weary. 'Come on, we'll go over to The Crack's and see these Satanists.'

'Fuck it anyway,' the young lad said.

Brendan Dunne, his young lad and Father Horsebox drove to The Crack's farm. The gate nudged open with a push of the bumper and they snail-rolled into the farmyard finding neither sight nor sound of a Satanist. The lights were all off in the house. Brendan cut the engine and they listened to it cool until The Crack ran across the farmyard towards them, naked as the day he was born, and because he was a person of short stature, the fear of God on his face looked fifty feet tall.

'What happened, Crack?' Father Horsebox asked but The Crack would never say, not to them, not to the sergeant, not to the Dublin homicide detectives when the Satanists, Willy Byrne and the geep were all dug up out of his silage pit.

'What happened that night, Crack?' asked psychiatrist after psychiatrist but The Crack was gone, long gone, wasting away in the corner of Phelan's pub when they eventually let him out, sinking pint after pint after pint.

Without solid explanation, there was nothing could be done but speculate. The story met somewhat of a cul-de-sac. There was nowhere for it to go but around and around, the gossip-hounds piecing it all together from the accounts of Father Horsebox, his housekeeper, Brendan Dunne and his young lad – bits being added, bits being taken away.

After the *Sunday World* exposé, Father Horsebox would spend his life vehemently denying the head Satanist was his son by the housekeeper and that they had hidden him away in a boarding school where he fell in with Satanists and being an illegitimate child of a priest, he'd quickly climbed the ranks. Father Horsebox avoided an excommunication by the skin of his very virile ballsack. Before Brendan Dunne died he claimed that The Crack was not naked, and there was no blood on him at all. But his young lad maintained he absolutely was naked and covered in blood. And a chainsaw suddenly materialised in the story. Some said this, some said that. The story would find a common ground until some bored and drunk gossip-hound went messing with it all over again.

Tom Phelan framed the photo of The Crack holding the geep then hung it on the snug wall. Those in the know said that the wall, they thought, was only for the dead. It was then the pub would look over at The Crack in the corner, festered, reeled and rattled, his black eyeball stare daring anybody to take one single step towards his dead mother in an attempt to fuck her and see what fuckin' happened, a blood-sodden rage in the way he carried himself, his sheep away perishing somewhere and his sheep be damned. And people realised the old Crack was dead and this new Crack was dangerous. The Antichrist maybe. And when people not in the know asked about the geep photo on the wall, the story would always begin the same – Willy Byrne with his fuck-your-mother swagger, a swagger to mug you off, a swagger to warn, were half a chance given, he would *actually* fuck your mother, a deed he had done to many a man of Ballybalt.

Green

Laura Surynt

1. The Foliate Head

She first saw him as she cycled home, on the corner of a building on the high street. He looked at her as she passed, and he continued to look as she slowed for pedestrians. But the day held a strange light, green and heavy with early spring, one of those late afternoons soon after the clocks change when the day seems to be longer than natural, and she thought it a trick of that light, and carried on, turning down a narrow road, forgetting what she'd seen. She saw him again in the corner of her classroom, after her students had left and an uncanny silence hung over the school. And then again, as a father of one of her students, sitting across from her, asking about exams and after-school revision and *Hamlet*, and then he wasn't. He flanked the archway that opened from the square into the church's garden, and was either side of the stone seat carved into the wall of the chapel, the seat the altar boys retired to after they'd swung the incense and held the candles aloft and alight all the way down the nave of the church. He sprang suddenly from a door in the wall of the lane she cut through on her way to Tesco to get limes and apples and instant porridge. He twisted from the smoothed timber, grained and dark. He was brown, then. He was blue in the mornings and gold in the evenings, features softened in stone. He was green, a spring kind of green, and then he wasn't.

Faye closed the front door and sat on the stairs to untie her laces. She could hear Anu in the kitchen making tea. She knew Anu knew she was home. Faye didn't say anything, Anu didn't say anything. She went upstairs and lay on their bed. She considered her day: a student had told her to fuck off when she asked them to take a seat, another punched a wall. Yesterday a boy had thrown a chair across the room as she took the register. She told him to leave the class, and sat calmly, pretending he was no longer there, and called the remainder of the names. Each student replied a polite here Miss, and, too, pretended the boy wasn't there. Faye smiled and asked them to turn to page thirty-eight. She launched into reading, the only thing she could do while they waited for the boy to leave. He didn't leave, he yelled and swore and ripped a poster off the wall. *Adverbial Phrases*. She read and read, she didn't stop for him. She read until he realised she was unreachable. He yelled fucking cunt on his way out, the fire door too heavy and slow to slam.

Faye thought teaching in this medieval town would be different from London, but it was the same. The school buildings were still falling apart, the class sizes too big. The students were hungry and angry. The teachers were tired.

She showered, washed her hair. She put on a shirt and jeans and went downstairs. She paused on the kitchen threshold until Anu finished her call and then went in.

Hi, she said.

Hi.

Who was that?

The hospital, someone's called in. Sorry, I've got to go back.

But you just finished a shift.

Anu shrugged.

Faye watched as Anu packed up her things. She watched as Anu drank the last of the tea and grabbed her keys from the table in the hall.

I'll be late, she said, don't wait up.

Through the front window Faye watched Anu unlock her bicycle. She swung her leg over and cycled off.

Faye woke then, later, now, and it was dark, but only just. She went out into the garden and felt the rumble of a passing train. She could see straight through the carriages and out the other side. Bodies silhouetted within. She thought of tomorrow. Tuesday. Six periods. She ran through the lessons in her head: *Beowulf*, *Macbeth*, Ted Hughes, *Jane Eyre*, George Orwell, *Hamlet*. She saw the marking pile on her desk, and the moderation documents. She counted on her fingers how many days she had until the data deadline. She counted on her fingers how many weeks until the school break. She rehearsed the phone calls she needed to make, she drafted emails in her head. She looked up and saw the sky was clear, dark. She felt sick. She began to cry. She went in and boiled two eggs and toasted two slices of bread. For the first time this year it was warm enough to eat outside if she wore a coat and hat. The bugs came, swarming the light of her phone. She read the news, she finished her drink. She went upstairs and fell asleep with the window open to the dark.

Faye had a meeting with Human Resources. She asked what was wrong. Faye tried to say but cried instead. She cried and cried and couldn't stop. The woman from Human Resources waited patiently for her to stop crying but finally left to speak to a colleague in the hallway. It's almost fifth period, she heard her say. Faye had a class fifth period, and sixth. She gathered her things and walked out of the room. She nodded to the two women who looked at her in dismay. She left the building and turned right towards the gates, not left and across the quad to her classroom. She cycled home. She went to bed.

2. The Disgorging Head

Faye woke and remembered something green from her dream. Something mossy, damp. She reached for it but found it fading. She knew it was him. It was already midmorning. Faye had been off work for a month now. She still felt it, the rhythm of the workday, as if it were burnt into her. She knew exactly where she would be standing right now, had she been at work, exactly what she would be saying, and she would be acutely aware of, exactly, how much time she had to teach what she needed to teach, until the bell rang, loud and true and final. She used to like how the bell sliced her day into neat segments to be consumed or spent teaching, marking, planning, meeting. Regardless of the light, the season, the day, the week, the bell rang and rang and rang. In July the three o'clock bell rang in the brightness. In January, the same bell rang as the sun was already setting.

She got out of bed and went downstairs. The clock on the microwave read 10:48. She made coffee and ate toast with butter and honey. She sliced a pear. She looked out the kitchen window and thought perhaps she might do some gardening, pull up the weeds. But then she thought not. Two birds, finches, landed on the thistles, grown tall in the grass. The thistles swayed a little with the weight of each bird but held true as the birds ate whatever seeds or pollen or bugs the plants had to offer.

Earlier, when Anu got up for her morning shift, she had asked Faye what she was going to do today. Sleep, go for a walk, maybe, Faye replied. Now, Faye opened maps on her phone and decided where she would go. There was a church in the countryside that she had never been to. It was away from town. She thought he might be there.

Faye walked for an hour before she could see the little church through the trees. Birch lined the path and nettles crowded the entrance. They brushed her bare legs as she walked in. In the cool of the interior she could feel the welts beginning to rise red. Faye knew she should go back outside and find a dock leaf to rub over the stings but she didn't. She knew he was here, the Green Man.

She thought perhaps he would be in the stained glass, but it hosted only neat diamonds, a few floral motifs, and a deep-blue cross. The sun was high, and the stone floor held washes of colour from the windows. Faye moved further into the church, waiting for her eyes to adjust. She studied the rafters, but they were just lengths of rough timber.

By now, she knew where to look – corners, adornments, carvings, chairs. But she couldn't see him, yet. She looked at the tiny free-standing organ, stepping back when she caught sight of her own face in a small mirror set into the veneer. In the reflection she saw the doorway of green illuminated in the gloom. He was there. She turned and saw him standing, staring. Above his head was the image she had missed, walked under without seeing. Where the two curves of the doorframe met his face was carved in stone – mouth open, two leaves of oak spilling out. And there he was too, not in stone, but something alive, a green bright kind of alive. The nettles that stung her grew from his legs and his chest was a trunk of some kind, knotted. The stone leaves were real now, glossy, and made up his face. He looked merry, he looked mocking. He stared at her and she tried to stare back, worried he would disappear. He didn't.

What are you doing here? she asked.

You came to find me, he said, taunting.

Fuck you, she thought.

Fuck you, he replied.

And then she knew she would, fuck him.

Suddenly, at that moment of thinking, she was standing in front of him. He was shorter than her, only by a little, and she could see the vines of his hair. He smelt of elderflower, of mushrooms, of rain. She placed her hand around his hip, slipping the other towards his lower back. He pulled her towards him and started licking her skin, his tongue a changing leaf. She didn't know which foliage was of his body and which was a garment, green and twisting, but she pulled pieces from him until he was soft green flesh, like a new shoot, smooth and fresh.

She reached her hand up between his thighs and held his penis – it was smooth too, and green, like a fruit of some kind. He grew hard and she put him in her mouth. Her eyes were closed but she could feel his pubic hair like moss, damp and fuzzy. He pulled her from the cold stone floor and he fucked her over one of the pews. One of her knees rested on the seat. He stood behind her, and as he came she tried to twist around – she wanted to watch what happened to him, the green the growing – but the pleasure was too much for her to focus and all she could see was his hand on her hip, all she could hear was the sound of his body against hers and the echo of her own voice on the stone.

After, they talked. He asked about the church, the windows. She read aloud the top leaflet from a neat stack on a small table at the entrance. He asked about the saints. What's a monastery? he asked. Who were the Saxons?

She told him, best she could, and they realised he knew it all, he was there, but didn't have the names.

Can you feel it, when you're put in stone, built into something, placed at an altar?

He didn't know what she meant.

Are you hungry? he asked, and for a moment she thought he'd magic up a bounty, push berries from his fingertips, an apple perhaps, but he didn't. He just got up and rifled through the cupboard under the bell tower stairs and returned with a tin of biscuits and a bottle of wine. He didn't eat or drink, just watched.

On the walk back she could feel the rise on her thighs where the nettles brushed against her skin. Anu was already home when she returned. That night, when they fucked, Anu said she tasted different.

How?

I dunno.

Bad different?

No, just different.

With her hands Anu felt the welts in the dark.

What did you do? she asked

Sometimes Faye went seeking him out, at others he appeared when she was not expecting him. Every time, she returned to the flat hot and jubilant and rumpled and scratched from brambles and thorns and leaves that had an edge sharp enough to cut. In early May she went a week without seeing him. She liked to walk for hours, to feel the early summer heat draw sweat from her body. She liked to be exhausted by the end of the day. It was on one of these days she noticed effigies over each door in a row of terrace houses. She climbed the steps to number thirteen, knocked, waited. He opened the door and she went in. Faye fucked the Green Man in those four houses over four days. Each house was slightly different from the next – a wall knocked through where it was solid next door, an attic loft, an extra bathroom or not – and he was slightly different in each house too, the same but changeable. She tried to see him change but couldn't. She only saw after the fact. On the second day, in the second house, he fucked her from behind, her hips bent over the windowsill, body leaning out to the street. She looked down and saw the stone and plaster effigy was gone, but the others, above the doors on either side and two doors down, were static, waiting, for her.

On the third day, in the third house, they spent the afternoon in the attic room. The room had a small bed and a small desk. This must be a student house, she said.

Faye asked where the bathroom was. He didn't know. It was downstairs and through the kitchen. She opened the frosted window and looked out into the overgrown garden. When she was done she found him in the front room, looking at all the books lining the wall.

What are they for? he asked.

What are what for?

These, he said, motioning to the shelves.

Reading, she said, they're books.

Books?

Yeah, books, they contain information or stories, distraction.

Distraction from what?

I dunno, life, work, this, she said, shrugging.

She found him one with pictures and opened it to show him. He held it close to his face and she watched his eyes scan the pages.

He was still reading when she left.

On the fourth day she noticed wisteria growing above the door of the first house. She hadn't noticed the vine when she first knocked, but she saw now it was heavy, tangled, smelling of sweet rot.

Windows open to the warm night, Faye couldn't sleep next to the restless Anu. It had been hot for weeks, this sweltering June heat. She rose and dressed, left the flat to walk off the sleeplessness. At this time of year the dawn came early, too early. It was just after four, the sky was lightening, and the buildings still held the heat of the day before. The town was empty, hushed, and as she wound her way through the cobbled streets she found him again and again – doorway, cloister, bridge. In the quiet stillness of the summer dawn she fucked the walls, the doors, the stone, the wood. He changed quickly now, under her touch, leaf and tree, flower, bud. She took in his thin green penis and then it grew and throbbed inside her. Pulling out she saw it was a deep green now, rough and wet.

3. The Bloodsucker Head

Faye couldn't see, she had something in her eye. A speck of dust, a piece of pollen. She rubbed it red before Anu pulled her close and stared into her eye. Anu licked her thumb and placed it on Faye's quivering eyeball. The pollen came free. It bloomed into flower, died, refolded in Anu's palm.

Faye had found them, Anu and the Green Man, having sex at the end of their street, Anu's back up against the stone, the Green Man pulsing through the seasons as he came inside her. Since then, Anu has stopped going to work too, and they have stayed home, having sex, sleeping late before roaming the town looking for him. The church is smothered in dog roses now, the bridge in brambles. Nettles are pushing their way up through gutters and drains. The four row houses that hosted those early encounters are overwhelmed by green. A hazel tree grows within one of them, heavy limbs pushing through the bay windows.

At first, the town tried to contain the green with lawnmowers, hedge trimmers. When that didn't work they rerouted the buses to avoid the places the Green Man had been. They closed the church for repair, moved the town council online. But, in their wandering, Faye and Anu have seen him with others too – the grocer, the doctor, a set of office workers fucked in quick succession. Each person ceased showing up for work, no explanation, only silence.

Faye walks through the cow parsley and goes downstairs. She finds Anu in the kitchen. Anu hands Faye a drink and leans against a young oak, still supple enough to sway under her weight. They pluck strawberries from bushes growing in the sink and eat handfuls of chestnuts from their neighbour's tree. A pond has sprung in their living room, and on its surface sit discs of green waterlilies and blue dragonflies. Outside a may tree throbs through the seasons – white blossom, green leaf, red berry, brown thorn.

The Second Can Wait

Sharmaine Lim

The first time Lianne heard her son call her mother-in-law 'Mama', she was sitting on the edge of her bed with the baby, Serene, clamped to her left breast. She usually kept the bedroom door closed when she nursed because her mother-in-law liked to come inside to watch, hovering just inches from the baby's face while the garlic on her breath putrefied on Lianne's chest. With a squeeze of Serene's thigh, she would complain, 'Aiyah, so skinny. I've told you already – what can your body make that's better than formula?'

But on that sun-baked Tuesday in August 1979, a heatwave seared across the island, eroding Lianne's willpower. Her mother-in-law's confinement rules didn't permit the opening of windows or the use of a fan. Wind was the enemy of the postpartum woman, even in the tropics. Lianne and Serene had been sweating like a pair of stewed plums in that tinderbox room day after day, while her mother-in-law cared for Tommy outside under the draught of a yellow box fan.

Although Lianne had stripped to her underwear,

her skin was molten, and she couldn't stop herself from scratching the blooms of heat rash in the folds of her groin. Serene wailed till her skin was splotched with pinpricks of burst capillaries. The sound made Lianne light-headed – so angry that she saw her hands hurling the tiny body against the wall to stop the crying. Shakily, Lianne wrapped a sarong around herself and opened the door. A welcome breath of air caressed her face, dispelling the image. Outside the bedroom was a pocket-sized living room with panels of aluminium louvres facing the communal corridor beyond. The metal burned in the glare of the afternoon sun, but it was cooler than the bedroom. Lianne put Serene to her breast, sank back and felt the milk let down.

As the baby suckled, Lianne flicked listlessly through the previous day's mail. Although she tried not to mind, it stung to hear Tommy babbling away in the living room while her mother-in-law interjected with indulgent replies. How things had changed in the two months since they'd moved in with Michael's mother. With no jobs, a toddler and a baby on the way, their abrupt return from England had left them with few options. And here she was, ten days after Serene's birth. Ten days of not being allowed to shower, wash her hair or step outside the apartment. The sociology books she had brought back from Oxford lay untouched on the floor. Only *Breastfeeding and Natural Child Spacing* was open, its arid advice a talisman against having another accidental pregnancy. A fug of musk seeped from every part of her – the pores on her skin, the weeping mound of pulverised flesh that used to be her vagina, her lank, greasy hair. Her perineal tears were not healing well. The stench seemed worse when she changed Serene's nappy. Together, they stank, cheesy notes of female bottoms entombed in a three-by-four-metre cell.

A bright-orange pamphlet caught her attention. Across the top were the words, 'The Second Can Wait' and below it, 'Girl or Boy, Two is Enough'. A picture of a couple and a little girl straddling a tricycle smiled back at her. The small print at the bottom read: 'Family Planning/Sterilisation Information Service. Call 538779 or go to your nearest Mother and Child Clinic'. It gave Lianne a turn, bringing to mind stories she'd seen in the *Guardian* about thousands of botched forced sterilisations in India during the Emergency. But surely such things wouldn't happen here?

'Mama, eat,' said Tommy. That wasn't right – she was *Ma*ma; the old dragon was *Ah* Ma. All thoughts of the pamphlet evaporated as Lianne's milk dried up. Serene choked and began to scream. Fighting the urge to shake her, Lianne forced her nipple into the gnashing, grasping mouth, wincing when the pincer gums drew blood.

At last, peace was restored, but Lianne could no longer hear Tommy. As soon as Serene's eyes began to glaze over, Lianne laid her down in her bassinet. A pair of thumbs pushed into the hollow of Serene's throat. Leaping back in alarm, Lianne looked at her hands. They were safely by her side. Serene was falling into a drowsy slumber, her splayed legs twitching like a frog's. Lianne rubbed her eyes. It was her sleep-addled brain, that's all it was. With unsteady fingers, she got dressed and tiptoed outside to look for Tommy.

The living room was furnished to match her mother-in-law's personality: a teak coffee table – all lethal corners and bowed, spindly legs; a settee upholstered in prickly tan fabric; a stereo cassette deck that randomly gave off micro electric shocks. In the kitchen, Tommy was seated in a highchair next to his grandmother, eating a slice of watermelon.

'Wow, darling, that looks yummy,' said Lianne, sliding into a chair beside him. At just thirteen months, Tommy hadn't yet lost the chubbiness of babyhood. The sight of his cheeks puffed full of fruit made Lianne yearn to pull him into her lap for a cuddle.

'All you do is hide in the room,' said Lianne's mother-in-law, rearranging her mouth into a scowl for her benefit.

Tommy pinched his nose with his fingers. 'Mama,' he said, giggling as he made a face.

Lianne laughed along, relieved to salvage her name, if not her dignity. Looking sidelong at her mother-in-law, she said, 'Ah Ma is being so kind to help Mama look after you. Make sure you leave some for her, OK?'

Lianne's mother-in-law reached over to the wall to switch off the fan. She was wearing her usual grey samfu, and the jade bangles on her wrists jangled whenever she moved. 'Do you think the dishes wash themselves?' she asked, pursing her lips. Like Michael, she had a slight underbite, but where his lower lip puckered attractively when he talked, on her, the effect was more like a sneer. 'Here, have some more, there's a good boy.'

Tommy seized another piece of watermelon and squeezed it till it crumbled into pieces. Cackling with delight, he offered Lianne a morsel. Lianne was just leaning forward to receive his gift when her mother-in-law jumped in.

'Naughty,' she chided, and shoved his hand away. 'No

cooling food for her.'

Tommy recoiled, looking chastened.

Lianne glared at her mother-in-law. But she bit her tongue at the thought of Michael's annoyance if his mother complained about her again. He often said how easy it should be for a Rhodes Scholar – or a former one at any rate – to follow a few simple rules. She flushed at the memory of the time he lost his temper because she refused to eat the foul medicinal brew his mother had made, claiming it would shrink Lianne's uterus. He had demanded that she get down on her knees and serve his mother a cup of tea to apologise for her disrespect.

'Lianne, fetch a towel to wipe his hands.'

Sulkily, Lianne got up to go to the bathroom. On her way, she paused at the window to gaze at the playground far below. A giant peacock slide presided over it; the preening sweep of its magnificent tail was studded with mosaics of indigo and emerald eyes. Surrounding the slide was a crescent of silver-white pelican spring riders. They had long, elegant necks and sensuous crimson bills, and their knobbly, webbed feet were pushed back as though they were about to fly away.

As Lianne dampened a flannel under the tap, she thought about the legend of the pelican who pierced her breast to feed her blood to her starving young – motherhood at its primordial best. Serene wasn't exactly starving, but she certainly bit hard enough to draw blood. No invitation needed there.

'Oy, what's taking so long? Where's the towel?'

Lianne hurried back to the table. With a huff, her mother-in-law snatched the flannel from her and made a show of cleaning Tommy's face. When she had finished, Lianne ruffled his hair, asking, 'Shall we read *Busiest People Ever?*' Tommy loved listening to stories about Huckle Cat and Lowly Worm. Her whole body was soothed by the touch of his cheek in the palm of her hand.

The old woman reached over to smooth down the hair that Lianne had fluffed up. 'We're going to watch *Tom and Jerry*, right, Ah Boy?'

Tommy clapped his hands enthusiastically and the old woman looked at Lianne with a triumphant gleam in her eye.

His name is Tommy, Lianne wanted to say. Ah Boy was what you used to call Michael. Just then, Serene began to whimper softly in the bedroom.

'Baby's hungry again?' Lianne's mother-in-law smirked. 'Your breast milk is like water, no wonder she cries all the time. You and your fancy Western ideas. Why don't you just give her a bottle?'

A burr of bitterness pressed into Lianne's gut. She watched her mother-in-law lift Tommy from his highchair and carry him into the living room. For the umpteenth time, Lianne fantasised about running away with her children. They would flee with just the clothes on their backs, a few books, and some nappies. No need for sterilised bottles and formula; her milk was in plentiful supply. Her mother-in-law had got things the wrong way round – it was precisely because she'd followed Western conventions and bottle-fed Tommy like all the other babies in Oxford that she'd fallen pregnant with Serene. If only she'd known about lactational amenorrhea, she would still be seven thousand miles away writing her thesis.

The first thing she would do when she ran away was to have a long, cold shower and wash her hair. Then she would eat all the things she loved. Her mouth watered at the thought of sinking her teeth into the delicate, pellucid flesh of a mangosteen and sipping a glass of freshly squeezed lime juice. She would have ice cream – huge brain-freezing scoops of red bean and sweetcorn, or even durian ice cream, though that would make her breath smell worse than her mother-in-law's.

'Lianne, baby's crying.'

'Yes, Ah Ma, I'm coming.'

'Lianne, Serene's crying,' said Michael in her ear.

She was deeply asleep on her back, dreaming of waving bluebells in Wadham's Cloister Garden.

'Lianne, get up.'

'Mm? I just fed her.' She dragged herself from the bluebells back to the dark, airless room. As Serene's cries built into full-blown hysterics, Tommy started to bawl too. Lianne sat up wearily, fumbling to massage her swollen breasts. The nipples were sore and cracked. 'Will you take Tommy?' she asked, reaching into the bassinet for Serene. A whiff of sourness escaped from her armpits.

'I need my sleep, you know I have an interview tomorrow,' mumbled Michael from the far end of the bed where he had retreated. On a four-foot-wide bed, the far end wasn't far at all, but he was trying his best.

'But I can't do both,' Lianne said over Serene's bellows. The baby arched her back, struggling against Lianne as she tried to guide her dripping nipple into her mouth.

'If you would just feed her before she wakes Tommy

up, this wouldn't happen,' said Michael. 'I told you we should let him sleep with my mother.' He stormed over to the cot and wagged his finger at him. 'Be quiet. Go back to sleep.' Tommy howled and rattled the bars of his cot.

'Michael, don't. It's not his fault.' Serene was feeding noisily now. 'Darling, lie down, it's OK,' said Lianne, motioning to Tommy with her free hand.

'Mama,' cried Tommy. He was standing in the cot and rocking on his heels in distress.

The doorknob turned, as if on cue, but Lianne was prepared for it. Her mother-in-law had a habit of barging into their bedroom at night whenever the children cried, and Lianne had wedged the back of a chair against the door before they went to bed.

'Everything all right in there?' Lianne's mother-in-law knocked hard on the door. 'I heard Ah Boy calling me.'

'He's not calling you –' said Lianne.

Michael groaned. 'How am I supposed to find better work if I'm up half the night tending to you lot? We don't have the luxury of two stipends anymore, Lianne.'

The pounding grew louder. 'You're waking up the entire neighbourhood,' shouted Lianne's mother-in-law. 'What will people think?'

Michael lifted Tommy and lay him down on his back. 'Stay,' he said firmly over his hiccupping. 'If you don't shut up, I'll put you outside with Ah Ma.'

Lianne gave Michael an agonised look. 'Ah Ma, everything's fine,' she called out, frozen in situ to avoid displacing Serene from her breast.

Michael went over to the door, removed the chair, and opened it a crack. 'Ma, you must take care and rest. Don't worry about us, we can manage,' he said in the mollifying voice he used only for her. He shut the door quietly.

Lianne couldn't help but feel a rill of satisfaction at the sound of the click. It was the first time he had taken her side against his mother even if he sounded like a mouse when he did. She missed having him all to herself; these days he seemed uninterested in anything she had to say.

She had first spotted him among the blur of blond and brown heads at the college MCR during freshers' week. She was drawn to the slim, bespectacled young man with the mop of wild black hair. Feeling unusually bold, she went to stand beside him at the bar, but found herself hopelessly tongue-tied. He turned to her with a smile and asked, 'Lianne, how are you finding your new digs?' – as though it was the most natural thing in the world to know the name of a girl he had just met. She had replied, 'I'll find it.' And then, because she hadn't the faintest clue what he meant, she asked, 'But what are we digging for?'

As Tommy's crying subsided, Lianne inched closer to Michael. She remembered how he used to put 10p coins into the pre-paid meter for the radiators in her college room even during the Trinity term because she felt the cold so much. He called her his frangible frangipani and teased her when she wore her gloves and hat indoors. Perhaps if she told him about the disturbing images she had been seeing, it would break their hold over her.

'I'm so tired. The interview is going to be a disaster.' He extracted his leg from under her clammy thigh.

She picked at the lint on Serene's Babygro, swallowing the ache at the back of her throat. 'Maybe a haircut might help?'

'Do you seriously think that will get me the job of my dreams? I'd rather stay at the back of the queue.'

She could tell that he was still smarting from being refused an interview with the civil service for having hair that covered his ears. The authorities were on a mission to stamp out hippie culture, and 'deviants' like Michael were always the last to be served, even at the post office.

'You know that isn't the reason I'm not getting offers.'

They said nothing more. Michael was right; his failure to get a proper engineering role had little to do with the government's social policies (even one as aptly named as Operation Snip Snip) and everything to do with him losing his Rhodes Scholarship. What a waste, the Warden had said when they confessed that they had gotten married without his permission and couldn't keep up with their studies now that a second baby was on the way. Lianne had only just started her DPhil. Green around the gills with morning sickness, she nearly threw up on his shoes as he lectured them about privilege and responsibility. Then he looked at her and said, 'I'm particularly disappointed in you, Lianne. You were one of our first women Scholars.'

'Michael,' she whispered into the darkness, 'I could get a job after the confinement. There was an ad in the papers for schoolteachers.'

'Who'll care for the children?' he asked tersely.

She felt a familiar vice tighten around her heart whenever he spoke like that. The one thing they argued over in the early days of their marriage was whose work should have priority. 'We could both apply for jobs, and if one of us does land something good, I'm sure we'd find a way,' she said, sounding more confident than she felt. Where was the man whose Panglossian resolve buoyed them through her first pregnancy?

He was silent for such a long time that she thought he had fallen asleep. Just as she was nodding off, he said, 'I'll be a kept man over my dead body. If you want to get a job, fine, I'll give Tommy to my mother. She's been asking anyway.'

Lianne bolted up in bed. 'What do you mean, give Tommy to your mother?'

He turned away and buried his head under a pillow.

At dawn, Lianne was woken by Michael's swearing. He had stubbed his toe and was stomping around the room slamming things while he got dressed for work. She pulled herself upright slowly. Although it was still early, the room was muggy, and a baste of sweat covered her skin. The last thing she wanted was another hot body glued to her side, but Serene needed to nurse. Michael left the room as soon as he could, taking Tommy with him. Lianne could hear her mother-in-law fussing over them in the kitchen. Every morning, she made congee garnished with gelatinous chunks of century eggs or fried dough sticks for their breakfast and would withdraw into injured silence if Michael dared to suggest that they preferred a slice of toast with jam.

Lianne kept the bedroom door slightly ajar, craving the sound of his voice. She would do anything to postpone the moment he left for work. Trapped with her mother-in-law and her ripe, fetid body, she no longer remembered what it was like to work in the Bodleian or feel the wind in her face as she walked along the canal paths on a brisk winter's day.

After Michael left, she kicked the door shut and lay down on the bed, too dejected to compete with her mother-in-law for Tommy's affection. Beside her, Serene lay, fed and quietly alert. Although Lianne felt guilty for keeping the silent truce between them, she avoided making eye contact so as not to set off another spree of demands. Overdue by two weeks, Serene had arrived heavy-boned with mottled skin and a pug-like expression carved into her face, as if the world owed her a great debt. Lianne didn't like to admit it even to herself, but Serene resembled Michael's mother so strongly that she had disliked her from the day she was born. She had harboured a hope that the name they gave her would beget a tranquil disposition, but how wrong she was. Whereas Tommy had fed obligingly, napped under the shade of a tree while Lianne buried her nose in research materials, Serene made everything a battle. Even her crying was pitched to vex like a drill hammering at her temple.

'Lianne, breakfast,' said her mother-in-law, pushing the door wide open. 'I've made pigs' trotters with black vinegar to increase your milk production. It's taken me hours – don't wait to be served.'

Serene broke wind and gave Lianne the evil eye. Kicking her feet in the air, her face turned florid, scrunching up in slow motion as she strained to open her bowels. 'Thank you, Ah Ma. I'll eat after changing Serene's nappy.'

By the time Lianne emerged from the room, her mother-in-law had taken Tommy downstairs to the playground. It was the perfect opportunity to switch on all the fans in the flat. Delirious with joy, she slipped a Queen cassette into the stereo. She stood with her arms held wide, swaying to

'Don't Stop Me Now' as her blouse ballooned in the wild gust of the fans. Afterwards, she went to the bathroom and changed her soiled maternity pad. On an impulse, she sniffed it, feeling the hairs on her arms tingle; it reeked of the fermented tofu that her mother-in-law often added to her porridge. All at once, Lianne saw herself dissolving into a miasma of quivering pigs' trotter stew, breast milk, and thick black clots of blood.

Peals of children's laughter floated up from below. She came out of the bathroom and looked out the window. Tommy perched precipitously at the top of the peacock's tail. He was motionless, as if suspended in fear, but moments later he pushed off and slid, squealing, down the slide. Confinement rules be damned, she was going to have a shower. She stepped back into the bathroom to remove her clothes but was immediately overcome with guilt. Michael was toiling away in a soul-destroying technician's job so they could have a roof over their heads and food to eat. The least she could do was get along with his mother. She might not have had a mother, but she knew what it was to be one. Glumly, she settled for a foot soak while continuing to watch Tommy. Her knees grew weak when she peered at the long bamboo poles of laundry jutting from the apartments below. It gave her a shiver to think of her mother-in-law falling out the window the next time she hung out their laundry.

'Someone from the government is here to see you. I told her she couldn't come in,' said Lianne's mother-in-law.

'Ah Ma, you turned away a government official?' Lianne went to investigate. In the corridor stood a woman wearing a brown tea dress. She had a cap of tightly permed hair much like a custard apple and arched, over-plucked eyebrows. 'Hello,' Lianne said through the metal slats, 'were you looking for me?'

'I told you it's not a good time,' shouted Lianne's mother-in-law from behind. 'She's in confinement, very dirty.'

The woman approached the window and took a clipboard from her briefcase. 'Are you Lianne Wong?'

'Yes. What's this about?' Lianne stepped back to spare the woman the ordeal of inhaling her body odour.

'I'm from the Ministry of Health, Family Planning. Did you receive our circular?' She shoved a piece of paper through the louvre.

Lianne recognised the orange pamphlet. It was the same as the one that had come in the mail.

'You have two children, correct?' asked the woman.

'She can't come outside, or her uterus will drop,' said Lianne's mother-in-law loudly.

The woman gave Lianne a withering look. 'Thomas and Serene, born only thirteen months apart?'

Tommy began whining and Serene's sirens cranked up inside the bedroom. Lianne's stomach tightened even as warm moistness spread across the nursing pads in her bra. She was desperate to go and feed the baby, but the woman was staring at her so intently that she dared not brush her off.

'Have you thought about when you will get sterilised?' asked the woman.

'She's very stubborn. Refuses to wear socks no matter how many times I remind her. The wind will get into her and give her arthritis,' said Lianne's mother-in-law.

Lianne could hear the collective tsking from the neighbours. Lowering her voice, she asked, 'I'm sorry?'

'Thirteen months is the smallest gap I've seen.' The woman stuck her pen through the window and tapped the top of the pamphlet as if Lianne had done something lewd. 'If you don't get sterilised, your children will be placed last during primary school registration.'

'And she can't even stack the dishes in order,' contributed Lianne's mother-in-law. 'But the worst thing is that she had a girl. So suay.'

'But I . . . I've just had the baby,' Lianne said weakly, the implication of the woman's question dawning on her. An image of Michael stepping into the shower behind her and cupping her breasts flashed before her eyes. It was the first time Tommy had slept through the night and she'd gotten up early to wash before waking him for his bottle. She and Michael had made love against the mouldy bathroom tiles, never once contemplating that the condom might fail. She had been surprised at how much she wanted him, how her body had responded with its own needs and appetites as though an escapee from the intoxicating, exhaustion-fuelled thrall of mother and child.

'Don't worry,' the woman said, suddenly smiling wolfishly. 'If you book with me, you can have the operation once you're out of confinement. It's a simple procedure.'

'But what if I use other contraceptive methods instead?'

The woman's demeanour darkened, and she put a big 'X' against Lianne's name on her clipboard. 'Then you'll pay more tax and lose priority in your public housing allocation. And if you get pregnant again, I warn you, the hospital fees will be much higher.'

Lianne hesitated, wondering if she should ask her about vasectomies. The breastfeeding book had cited a study showing that it was less invasive than tubal ligation. 'Do men ever get sterilised?'

'What?' The woman shook her head incredulously and made a snipping gesture. 'They think it will make them less manly.' Pressing her lips together sympathetically, she continued, 'I'll be back in two days. Make sure you sign the form.' She nodded to Lianne's mother-in-law and clacked away towards the stairs.

That night, after the children had fallen asleep, Lianne showed Michael the pamphlet. 'They want me to get sterilised, but I'm worried about it going wrong. I've read that vasectomies are safer.'

Michael frowned. 'This morning's interview was a car crash, Lianne. We're going to need two salaries to make ends meet. After the confinement, my mother will take Tommy, and Serene can go to a neighbour in the next block.'

The resignation in his voice unsettled Lianne. It felt like both an admission of defeat and a punishment. But who was being punished – she or the children? Was it unreasonable to feel upset that Tommy would be cared for by his own grandmother? The prospect of having her body and mind back made her giddy, though whether it was with anticipation or fear, she couldn't tell. Either way, the children shouldn't be separated. 'Will Ah Ma consider taking Serene as well?' They could be a dyad, tandem nearly-twins who would always have each other. Her very own sociological study.

'You know what she's like. Only boys count.'

Lianne looked over at Serene sadly. I'm sorry I'm such a rubbish mother, Lianne telepathed to her daughter, watching her mouth making little moues in her dreams. On the dome of her cheek was a brown smear of blood. Lianne thought of the mother pelican's sacrifice. Did she differentiate between male and female chicks? I'm sorry I brought you into this world before we were ready for you. She imagined Serene growing up, vying with her brother for attention, always coming second. Then as a young woman, falling in love, marrying, having babies, making impossible choices like so many before her.

'What about the sterilisation?' she asked.

'I suppose you'll have to fall in line.' He took off his glasses and pinched the bridge of his nose.

It dawned on her that he wouldn't cut his hair short but was prepared to let her be sterilised. She had been hoping he would offer to have a vasectomy, or at least weigh up which procedure was safer. Shaking her head, she took the leaflet from him and switched off the bedside lamp.

She lay awake in the dark for hours clawing at her itchy scalp. Her whole head seemed to be on fire. Sometime in the early morning, before Serene could rouse everyone with her clamours for a feed, Lianne got out of bed. She swaddled Serene in a sling against her chest. Tommy smiled sleepily and put his arms around Lianne's neck as she cocooned him in another sling beside his sister. When all the knots of fabric had been tied, the children's bodies cleaved to her and their sleeping faces touched, cheek to cheek.

She hugged them tight, hunching over as she crept to the front door. Anaemic light from the corridor outside bled across the walls and ceiling of the living room. At the threshold, Lianne looked back over her shoulder. Her shadow loomed over them, a lumpy three-headed ogre. It was the first time she had held the children together in her arms. They came from her, both of them. A body deformed of form but brimming with life. She straightened her shoulders, stretching to her full height though the pressure on her engorged breasts was like burning coals and her vaginal stitches bit into her flesh. Nobody was going to take her babies from her or tie up her tubes.

Out the front door she inched, her mother-in-law's dire predictions ringing in her ears. Her uterus stayed intact. She took another cautious step. When crippling arthritis did not strike her down, she began waddling towards the lift lobby. A gentle breeze kissed the welts on her scalp. On the way down, the lift reeked of urine but she hardly noticed. As she strode into the warm night, the scent of newly cut grass filled her with euphoria. She hastened towards the playground. Coming to a stop in the shadow of the slide, she felt the children stir and lift their heads. The peacock towered over them, its jewelled train glittering in the amber cast of the streetlamp. But it was not the peacock that held Lianne's attention, it was the pelicans. Here at last, she was in the presence of the fantastic beasts. Blood-red beaks opening wide, breasts proud, their majestic wings folded high against their backs, poised to take flight. From behind came hurried footsteps. Michael and his mother were shouting for her. With great care, she climbed onto the back of the largest bird and began to rock in slow, pendulous motions as she and her babies soared, laughing, into the sky.

A Love Story

Karishma Jobanputra

We ate everywhere.

We ate at New York restaurants priced like New York restaurants, our first date at a place that had thick, white tablecloths and candles that looked like tea lights but sexier, and it would have been an affront to the aesthetic if we did not order several glasses of wine, $25 a glass, each. Another night, a place on Prince Street that was *trendy*, not *fancy*; we sat at the granite bar, opposite a tandoor oven, because we hadn't made a reservation. Rosemary naan and paneer curry, the cheese made in-house, a fenugreek and tomato sauce. It delivered better daal and chai than even my mother could make. Can you believe that? I asked you, laughing. Can you believe I would even say that? She'd kill me if she heard me! Of course, she'd kill me well before I got to those words if she knew who I was with, the boy I was about to start falling for – American, white, aspiring musician. You smiled, hand on my knee, hand on my thigh. Good job she can't. We downed one, then another, then another Hangin' Out with Ravi Shankar (gin, gin, gin, too much gin), another Shankar, yes, we said, yes, thank you, yes. Stumbled to the subway, hand around my waist, on my shoulder, cupping my cheek. Then, standing in the Midtown bar you used to work at, where everybody loved you, and there were chandeliers dripping light like ribbons, streaking down your face like tears. They have mac and cheese, you said, voice deep and honeyed in my ear, ordering it from your friend who in a few weeks would be my friend, too.

Days later, I made us oatmeal for dinner in my thumbnail of a kitchen deep in Crown Heights. You said you liked it, but there were still banana pennies and peanut butter clumps in your bowl, and I didn't believe you. Red wine does not pair well with oats, I said, and opened it anyway. I didn't have a couch yet, couldn't afford one, but the floor was more comfortable than we both imagined. Sex on the floor is better than sex on a bed because it means you couldn't stop yourselves in time to make it to the bedroom. Then, a slew of places priced reasonably, places, now, that were no longer designed to impress me but to show me who you really were, what you really liked. The Irish pub where I pretended to eat oily onion rings from plastic baskets and threw back lukewarm beer, ignored stomach cramps that grew out of my anxiety about calories and the feeling that the oil was dripping down my chin, smiled at friends of yours I didn't know and who were not easy to talk to. The guys only wanted to talk to you, their girlfriends cold-eyed and rude-faced. We went clubbing with better friends with better girlfriends, to a bar in a basement, to a shisha lounge, to a club lit red, hot with bodies and roving eyes. More beer, more gin, salty tequila, and then someone's apartment with an NBA game on – chips, dip, jalapeño liquor. Later, bad and therefore good dollar pizza on Bleecker Street (or perhaps MacDougal, the gin was too much, again) at 3 a.m., a cold cheese-and-pasta-topped slice to soak up the spirits in my stomach like we were real New Yorkers who swallowed carbs like water because we were and it was gorgeous, being this drunk and this free. I know you're from London, you said, but you're a New Yorker really, and perhaps it was this moment I fell in love with you, too much food forcing the top button of my jeans open, worries about feeling thin floating away like moths towards the light. Spring found us in the form of the snow cone cart just blocks from the Whitney, a berry flavour that turned our tongues blue, the heat of the day and the cold of our tongues threading through the sunlit days until summer overtook us. Warm nights, waking up next to you more often than not, tripping over your dead-to-the-world body to find water in your fridge. Heat, the kind that screamed New York City. Coarse and wet, a constant undertone of the smell of garbage that I associated with the West 4th Street subway station.

One afternoon, you piggybacked me from Vanderbilt to Nostrand because my new shoes were giving me blisters, and we burst into my apartment, slammed open the window and stripped down to our underwear, barely chewing our bagels because we were ravenous, coughing because the fizz of San Pellegrino got stuck in our noses. White bra, flower skirt at my feet. You looked at me and knocked the everything bagel from my hand, carried me to the bedroom. We ate more bagels – yours pumpernickel with cream cheese, mine everything with tofu and scallions and tomatoes and capers. My favourite place was right by your apartment, near the N train, a place with an unoriginal, nondescript name and bagels the size of my head, spread thick with avocado, and TVs on the walls playing *Friends* on repeat. Breakfast, lunch, brunch on the weekend. On your birthday, we got almost everything on the menu at Sarabeth's because you really loved *Gossip Girl* and they went there that time, remember? Serena and Blair? I know, I laughed back at you, piled the food I couldn't eat onto your plate. I could not imagine loving someone else. One fall night, the crispness suddenly around us, I texted you: *Meet me at By Chloe*. You: *This place is* vegan? You left, messaged me to meet you at a bar that went by the name Tavern nearby because you needed a real burger. I was angry until I beat you at darts and pool. You bought me beer after beer, but I kept winning, and you found it funny, not annoying. You cooked steak with pomegranate that I refused, I scrambled eggs for breakfast that you declined. I was vegetarian, you weren't keen on eggs. You didn't like too much cheese, picked it off your pizza, and then I ate it. Didn't finish a cookie because there were too many chocolate chips and they were too big; I ate those, too. You didn't scrape out all the black beans from the can once, so I ate those, straight from the can, and you were disgusted, the corner of your mouth curling up like baking parchment. Let me cook it for you, you said, stirring beans into a pan with some onions, garlic and peppers, calling it soup. This is perfect, I said, and you softened and said, rolling your eyes at the cliché of it but saying it still, No, that's you.

You swallowed too-large sandwiches stuffed with meat and I was disgusted. Gabagool, you said. I'm Italian, you said, Queens accent strong. I went to Van Lleuwen in the West Village alone when I realised we were down to just a few months, six months, until my visa ran out – the amount of time we'd already had, and I knew at this point that I was hopelessly in love with you. Could I do this –

this whole us thing, this whole you're-not-Indian thing, this whole I-have-to-move-back-to-London thing – and survive? I didn't know, didn't want to know, ate chocolate ice cream with chocolate sauce and felt like a child again, and then felt sick, sick sick sick to my stomach, because my teeth ached from sugar and sadness and uncertainty and wondering about ending it. Wondering about going back to my apartment, not yours, to never go to yours again. I threw up the ice cream on the side of the street, sweet vomit burning my throat, and then I went to your apartment, let myself in with the key you gave me so casually the day before, and fell asleep in your bed, waiting for you to come home from a gig in the faltering early hours of the morning. We ate at Salumeria Rosi on the Upper West Side, a tiny place that doubled as a salami counter and charged too much for a main. There we ate hearty gnocchi and a strange dessert with bacon, even though we'd asked for chocolate mousse. It was just OK, my fork poking around like a nervous mouse, trying to avoid the meat. I'd decided to end it, but the words wouldn't come, lodged in my throat like stubborn apple seeds, potato causing my stomach to spill over the top of my low-rise trousers, refusing to be reined in, my brain wanting to scoop out my insides and burn them. That was when the need came back stronger than it had in months, the deep need to feel empty, to *be* empty, to feel the comfort of a finger scraping at the raw and sensitive inside of my throat. As you paid the bill, I realised it was too late, realised I had found someone to love and couldn't let go of, realised I was jumping off of something I knew and onto something I didn't, and I was mid-air, there was no turning around, and I held your hand instead of giving in to what my throat was calling out for.

We shared a mushroom fig pizza from Emily's, the pizza place famous for its burgers, while you explained the basketball that was happening on the screen, and I told you I didn't care and kissed you so you didn't either. The server asked, a glint in his eye, if we were newlyweds. We ate cheap, spicy ramen in the East Village when I had a cold and then expensive, salty mozzarella sticks at Bryant Park when I didn't. We ate mounds of rice and creamed spinach and too-spicy curry (mine potato, yours goat) at a tiny Indian place in Long Island City that New York foodies were raving about, but I thought was fine and nothing more. Nothing on my mother, I said. I'd like to meet her, you replied. I shrugged, pretending it was a possibility, kept looking over at you, confused by your face that was bare without a beard. I'm trying it out, you said. I hope you stop, I didn't say, feeling strongly but not enough to hurt your feelings. We ate blueberry Eggo waffles in the mornings, chocolate chip Little Bites that were shiny with grease in the afternoons, and Smucker's peanut butter straight from the jar in the pink, burgeoning hours, the fridge door open, harsh, artificial light outlining our fingers fumbling first with condiments, with the copper-coloured filter purifier your roommate adored and then, desperately, with my bra and your belt. All of this, looking at each other and not the looming future when I would have to leave, five months, now four, now three.

We drank cold diet cream soda and Thai iced tea; gin shots to forget, carrot juice in the morning to remember we had to keep going. More gin and tonics with your friends, ones that were easy to talk to this time at a pool bar by

Union Square where we laughed until 2 a.m., 3 a.m., 4 a.m. They like you, you told me. I like them, I told you back. Other nights we ate takeout pizza in bed but really were just there for the greasy, parmesan-topped garlic knots. Months later, I would leave, move back to London, and I would dream of those spirals of dough, the butter and oil on my mouth like lip gloss. Months later, I would cry, missing the pungent garlic, the slick grease, the throwaway words that we used so easily, love and babe. Months later, I'd remember the Saturday morning we woke, bleary-eyed, the day we started counting in weeks, not months, and had sex over and over and over again like one of us was dying, until we staggered to the kitchen, starving, and waited impatiently for a whole pack of frozen pizza pierogis to cook, perfuming the kitchen with the smell of cheese and tomato. We sautéed garlic and onions in butter while we waited, and the air crackled with heat and fat. When they were done, we dipped them in sriracha, and I burnt the roof of my mouth. Too hot, too hot, too hot. I ate too quickly, too much, it was all too much, and ran to the bathroom. You held me when I told you. All this time, you said, I didn't know. I nodded and said it had been getting better, that I was sorry. You said there was nothing to be sorry for, that your sister had bulimia, you understood, was I relapsing, was I scared of something. You didn't mean to ask, but it slipped from your mouth, you knew what I was scared of, what was coming for me and for you – for us. You waited for hours until I fell asleep so I wouldn't overeat and then vomit, wouldn't succumb to old patterns that still felt normal, wouldn't fall, wouldn't lose myself to an old self that told me: Don't eat, stuff a finger down your throat, eat

eat eat don't don't don't. You tipped coffee into my mouth one morning at Nostrand Avenue subway station, tears bubbling under closed eyelids because I was having a bad day, could feel time ticking in my pulse, was too afraid to swallow anything. You waited until the commuters got on the train you needed, then parted my lips and said, Just one sip. I love you, I said, the stench of urine around us, and swallowed.

I started eating hunks of pineapple and fistfuls of overpriced strawberries because my roommate said they make it taste better down there, and I wanted the end to be sweet. Down there? I asked her. Down there, she said knowingly and winked. You ate BLTs with avocado from the deli on my block. I ate the edges of those BLTs from the deli on my block, stole the avocado and crust like a bird, and you raised your eyebrows. I can just get you a sandwich, you know. I'm not hungry, I said, and you looked at me, unspoken questions in your eyes. It's not that . . . I just . . . I want yours. You smiled. Then there was green rice and green juice, falafel and kimchi because I was very Brooklyn, and good independent-coffee-shop coffees and bad diner coffees and worse, mediocre coffees that still cost more than $6. We held hands, and you didn't let me go to the bathroom after we ate. We tried vegan burgers and red pesto, coffee that burnt a hole in your stomach and made you shaky and scared. There was the drunken promise of McDonald's that never happened, and I got so angry, so irate because I'd had too much gin, then tequila, then vodka, and was so end-of-the-world *hungry*. I just want a hash brown, oh my *God*. That tone from me again at Monte's in the Village, eight weeks to go, an evening I felt bloated and rageful that you would pick Italian though, of course, I said pick whatever you want, and so you chose Italian, a cuisine heavy on carbs and cheese, and I was just so tired of not being *well*, of having something wrong with me and food, of needing you to stop me from forcing sustenance out of myself, of this expired visa hanging over us like a spectre and an end in sight. Standing outside while you wondered what you'd done wrong, I called home, miles and miles away, and my mum asked, Are you OK? and I didn't know what to say. She said, Eat something and apologise to whoever you need to apologise to. I did only one of those things – the pasta bulging in my mouth, painfully starchy – and then cried, letting you think something was your fault. You didn't understand and waited for me to tell you, a week later, that I was sorry. You said it was OK, eyes sad, brow heavy.

There were countless tubs of pomegranate you wouldn't share, and I didn't want, jewels to you and tiny blood vessels to me. There were the boiled dumplings I forced you to try at the Union Square Christmas market, which we scarfed down, felt them slide down our throats, burning hot, as our noses turned numb from the cold; potato and steak and mushroom with fried sauerkraut and slick sour cream. We went to Jazz at Lincoln Centre, my Christmas present to you, and I picked out the green, yellow and blue M&Ms and handed you the rest, leaning forward to see the show. You ate them because you were staunch in your belief that all the colours tasted the same, and also, they were extortionate; we would not be wasting them. There was Earl Grey ice cream, and crunchy waffle cones, and hot fudge sauce that we got for free because the lady behind the counter could tell I was fanatic about hot fudge. After we ate it and became her friend, she gave me an espresso cup of hot fudge, and I hugged her. There was the time I cried because I wanted hot fudge more than anything and then, when we got to the front of the line at the Big Gay Ice Cream shop, they were all out. You wouldn't let it go, and they found some somehow, but I refused, stubborn and angry. You got angry, too, slammed the bedroom door when we got home, and said you just wanted to make me happy. I want to be happy, too, I said, tears glistening, warping my image of you, and neither of us slept that night, our insides hot and angry and tired.

We ate holding each other, on your beanbags and at my Craigslist coffee table, outside at the Hungarian Pastry Shop where writers wrote books, where I hoped I might one day finish mine, and at a Mexican restaurant in Williamsburg after a good (my opinion) / bad (your opinion) black-and-white movie at 2 a.m. We talked about it on the subway home, and a guy looked at us, Are you talking about *The Apartment*? We nodded. That movie *sucks*. I rolled my eyes. You high-fived him, are still friends with him now, I think. There were chocolate cupcakes from Magnolia Bakery because they were out of banana pudding, there were ice cream dates at Ample Hills, where you always chose the wrong flavour, and Chemex-brewed cinnamon coffee on those dwindling Sunday mornings. I ate a portion and a half of pasta your stepdad made for us for dinner – and found myself unbelievably worry-free about the fact that my stomach was bursting, clutching your hand under the table – pasta he and your mother then gave me to take home and I ate for days after. Penne with lots of olive oil and yellow squash that I picked out, wanted to save alongside a certain glow that came with the feeling of knowing your family liked me. The glow when you showed me the text from your stepdad: *We really like her, don't mess it up.* We ate homemade brunch one time after I convinced you eggs were good, stacked English muffins with runny yolks, added soft avocado, mushrooms, peppery rocket, cheese, and more sriracha. Burnt the roof of my mouth again. A single tofurkey sausage; you didn't like it. We ate creamy coconut milk curry with potatoes and wilted spinach when we cooked to save money. Knobbly brown rice, my knuckle nicked on the lid of a can of crushed tomatoes. You rummaged around for a tiny plaster, one of the many I had given you because I learnt you didn't have any in the house, and it made me nervous. Hershey's chocolate pudding, not rich enough for my liking, in the early hours of the morning while I inhaled the harsh cigarette smoke from the Marlboro Reds your roommate was smoking. Smoke I tried to eat, the gorgeous wisps wrapped around my tongue, curls that tasted like Paris and brisk autumn mornings. And the metallic, dry taste, too, of the sex that would come after we finished playing poker on your faux-leather couch that was littered with dimes and nickels and quarters. You invited them, your roommate and his girlfriend, to my surprise birthday brunch. Gossip Coffee, the place right by your apartment that did hazelnut pancakes with edible glitter and irrationally large sandwiches; the place I posted about on social media, and when people asked me, *WHERE IS THIS??????*, I'd say I didn't remember because I was keeping it close to my chest, saving it as one of *our* things. Please, all of you, fuck *off*. This is *mine*.

I ate free fries, some crispy and some despicably soft at the bar you worked at. They were waiting for me every time I walked in, before I even said I wanted anything. Swallowed the seed of anxiety that germinated from that old self fearful of potato, and it died completely when you brought me mayonnaise as well as ketchup. Mayonnaise made you nauseous and made me happy. Thanks, I whispered in your ear.

We ate vegan oat pancakes that I loved making, and you realised you loved eating. You ordered pineapple ice cream even though you didn't want it, but I did, the bustling market of Reading Terminal around us on our day trip to Philly, and I teared up with thanks because I didn't have the strength to say, I want ice cream – too afraid, still deep in an old fear that I would force myself to the edge of the toilet bowl even though the need to do it was always lesser when I was with you. On the empty Greyhound back to New York, you looked at me mischievously and said, I wonder what it tastes like down there now, after all that pineapple, and I told you to find out, the dark empty bus trundling along, no witnesses except the bus driver who was too far away to know what was going on. We ate in your bed, bad Chinese food balanced on a chair doubling as a table in your bedroom that smelled perpetually of pot and sweat. We ate as we yelled over Thai food at my favourite place in Prospect Heights on Valentine's Day, forever fighting about politics. We ate Mexican appetisers at my best friend's engagement party in some part of Gowanus I had never been to, the sky electric purple with thunder, a weepiness in the air because these were the last few moments, they had come around now, and I was squeezing my eyes shut, pretending pretending pretending that I wasn't about to leave. I realised you would stay here and I would not, you could see these friends that were actually mine, and I could not. We found pizza nearby at a place with checked tablecloths, then stumbled to a bar in Cobble Hill, reuniting with the happy couple drinking too many beers, the front of the bar completely open and letting in violet flashes of light and the heady smell of rain. I took you to A Salt & Battery and also Tea & Sympathy, to let myself imagine maybe one day we might both be in London. You took one look at the mushy peas, the haggis, the very fat chips and told me I was insane. You're perfect, you said, except for the fact that you think this is good. Just try the scone, I said, and you grimaced. I guess this is what love is, you replied after nearly choking on a sultana, and I threw my hands up in defeat and ordered us both gin and tonics – doubles, I told our waitress – at the pub next door.

In the last week, we ate in silence, with Nicki Minaj playing, with your friends and my friends, with only each other, with strangers around us at Prospect Park. We went back to the dive bar we found in those first few months of us, right at the beginning when you had looked at the menu and asked if I wanted to get both mac and cheese and fries to share, and I could have said I love you there and then if I wasn't so afraid or so unaware that that was what that feeling was, or so convinced that it was stupid to think I could feel love just because you asked me if I wanted both fries and mac and cheese because, of course, I did, and just needed you to ask me; I was happy and I could eat anything and everything in that moment. We ate with *Gossip Girl* in the background and then in the foreground and before sex and after sex and outside in the cold weather and inside in my stuffy Brooklyn apartment. We made lists of places to take each other, things to try when I came back because, of course, you said, you'll come back, and we have to be prepared. Levain cookies pending, Rahi in the Village pending, Rubirosa, Parm, Bodrum, Roberta's, all pending, all on the list.

We ate when we were hungry and when it was time, on Thanksgiving and on Valentine's Day, in Brooklyn and Queens and Manhattan, on park benches and sidewalks. We ate like we didn't care about what we ate, but sometimes like we did, like we didn't look at prices, but sometimes like we did, like it mattered where or what we ate and also like it didn't, like we were happy and hungry, like we were thrilled to be alive and were famished, having just found each other. We ate like we were in love. Like every time we got to do this, we were doing something to remember, doing something defiantly, our bodies holding this thing, this us, like it might fly away, evaporate into something indiscernible above a loud city stuffed with food that would go on, with or without us, and if we kept going like this, perhaps somehow we would outrun the future and its sadness. And if we didn't manage that, as we didn't, we realised, the city flashing past us, at least we would remember the food, at least we might manage to remember the things that made us, that kept us going.

At JFK, you wore the checked three-quarter trousers I hated. You held me and we tasted salty tears. I walked through Security, and I ordered a wholemeal bagel priced like a tin of caviar, called you to tell you I loved you, took a bite, spat it out into a thin napkin. Sat down on the ground, waited for something to happen, waited for the clenched bread in my hand to disappear, for it to become gin or pizza or your hand, for the need to run to the toilet to evaporate, for the fear that it never would – not without you – to die down, for the need to let our time come up and out of my throat to be flushed away, waited for all of the food to stop coursing through my body and heart and brain, for our list of pending places to come alive and take me back, to close my eyes and open them anywhere that wasn't here. For our love story to keep going.

Keiko and I

Rosie Chen

It was October, and it smelled of rain. The door of the café opened, ushering a gust of wind inside, which rippled through the pages of Cathay's *Cosmopolitan* and revealed flashes of baguette bags, tinted moisturisers and colourful strap-ons.

The magazine fell open at the OnlyFans article that I had glanced at over Cathay's shoulder while I played on my phone. The woman who was featured in the article wore John Lennon-style glasses. She had quit her office job the year before. Her plain, proud parents ran a hotel pub in Gloucestershire.

'That girl has the same glasses as you,' I said.

Cathay scoffed. 'She makes more money in two months than I do in a year.'

Cathay was a book editor. She was smart and sympathetic on Twitter. At university, she had dreamed of writing a novel. 'What happened to your novel?' I once asked. Cathay frowned. A sudden foul smell. 'I've found my calling,' she told me. 'You know how competitive jobs in publishing are.'

Later, 'I'm more satisfied than most writers, trust me.'

A good life was like good code, easy to read.

I did not have a calling.

I was the only developer I knew who had no desire to build my own games or applications. It pleased me to imagine how easily I could let all my technical knowledge slip away, like the French I had learned at school.

'Maybe I should get on OnlyFans,' I said. 'I would make more money than Simon on OnlyFans.'

I had recently found out that my male colleague, Simon, was being paid seventeen thousand pounds more than me to do the same job. I slept with him, and he told me. An out-of-cycle pay rise. He had threatened to quit, to go to a competitor. The guy who I had done mostly doggy with, throwing his weight around.

I had chosen him because I believed he was devoid of ego. Quietly competent, a little tragic. He carried a messenger bag. He liked writing technical documentation. He attended all my lunch-and-learns, and diligently worked through the exercises.

We had finished our breakfasts in silence. He told me I was scaring him, and I was glad.

'Unless Simon was catfishing as an Asian woman,' said Cathay.

We both laughed. Cathay found the page that she had lost, an interview with an actress who was already ten years younger than us. I returned to my phone, and began to wonder, and scrolled until my vision blurred.

My best friend before Cathay was my older brother, Michael.

We ate McDonald's on our knees and elbows. We watched *Robot Wars*. We had retractable roller shoes before everyone else, from China. Our parents had left China in the 80s. They were, literally, children of the Revolution. They loved us too much to let us want more than what we had.

We had scholarships for private schools. We had music lessons. We had a computer, over which we fought bitterly.

Michael called me from Oxford. It was late, the moon high above our childhood home. He vomited, a brown sound, and announced that he had just lost his virginity. I asked, and she was white. 'Are you proud of me?' he kept asking, and I insisted I was. By the end, we were both in tears.

One day, our parents would die, leaving us to it.

At private school, I followed white girls around like a wasp. I was not allowed to go to their parties. I masturbated over their pictures on Facebook, and blamed my parents for everything.

I met Cathay at Cambridge. I surprised us both by losing my virginity before her, to a fourth-year called Bryce. Cathay did 'everything but' for a while. She lost her virginity to a second-year at our college called Rob Less. He was friends with Pilly Polly, who loved pills and had been in the year above me at private school.

'Rob Less only slept with you because he has an Asian fetish,' said Pilly Polly. She was drunk, we all were. When I told her that it wasn't me who had slept with Rob Less, she only laughed. Later that year, we made out. She was dressed as 'the future', iridescent strips of tin foil flowering from the waistband of her skirt.

I gained a reputation for being a 'dark horse', an epithet which Cathay and I decided, in the end, was racially loaded.

But what did I expect?

And wasn't Chinese practically white?

'You are top of the class,' said my mother, as though I'd only forgotten, when the boys at school were calling me fugly. Also, 'frying pan'. Because my face was so flat, it must have been smashed by a frying pan.

I was no longer top of the class, at Cambridge.

'You're the worst drunk I know,' Cathay told me, often. I moaned like a goat. She had other friends, over a thousand friends on Facebook. But it was me who she wore home at the end of the night, peeling me off the floor like a label with her name on it.

Her name was supposed to be 'Cathy', but her mother, Brandie, had misspelt it at the hospital. Brandie was Chinese-Chinese, from Guangzhou. Cathay's father, Eddie, was from the East End, originally from Hong Kong. When Cathay was thirteen she had surgery for an atrial septal defect. Her parents were never the same after that. Every day, 'I love you.' Every day, 'What makes you happy?'

The inspiration, I recalled, for the novel she never wrote.

Cathay went on dates. Cathay wore red lipstick and silver hoop earrings and skirts made of plastic. Cathay lay on her front on my single bed and copied Latin sentences out of fusty hardbacks, chewing her nails, complaining about white people.

It was Cathay who I called from the women's bathroom after my meeting with Veronica. Veronica was my manager, and Simon's. 'EVERYTHING – I – DO – IS –

POINTLESS,' I told Cathay, choking into a noodle of toilet paper. I regurgitated Veronica's non-apologies about frozen budgets, valued contributions, rumoured redundancies.

If I continued to do good work, I'd probably be safe from redundancy, but I wasn't getting a pay rise.

'You still earn a lot,' said Cathay. 'More than – most people on the planet.'

I would never forgive her for saying that. Because she was right, of course. And the company had been under no obligation to tell me they had increased Simon's salary.

I told Cathay that the book launch she was attending that evening sounded super fun! And then I returned to my desk. I stared at the time on my computer until it changed into something I couldn't recognise. I beamed at Veronica when I passed her in the hallway, smiling with my mouth shut, not wanting her, or anyone else, to pity me.

After a cursory Google search, I decided to ask Christine for help.

Christine was Chinese-Chinese. She had been my college mum. Someone once told me that her family was one of the top ten richest in Asia. But I checked the Forbes list, and couldn't find them.

At private school, I was believed to be a Chinese genius. But only because I studied constantly, and had already learned calculus from my parents. Christine was a real Chinese genius. Incidentally, she also worked hard.

Christine, hey! How are you??

Lol, fine. What's up?

Christine never messaged first. But if she was online, she replied instantly. I messaged on her birthday, which was 9/11, and on Chinese New Year. Mostly, I messaged about work.

Her profile picture looked like coffee art, but was in fact an abstract oil painting. A blushing brown smiley. A Chinese-Chinese thing. My mother's profile picture was a pine tree, alone on a hill.

> *I'm trying to create a completely fake person,*
> *like multiple different pics with the same face*
> *Lol why? Catfish?*
> *No . . . . . .*

Christine lived in San Francisco and worked at a machine learning startup. Before that, she had worked at Facebook. I had a job interview at Facebook in my fourth year. *Mark Zuckerberg's wife is Chinese*, messaged Cathay. *I think that will work in your favour.*

Her degree was over before mine. She had moved back to London, where she lived for free with her parents, and complained that she was underpaid, and ridiculed me for every corporate job I applied for.

> *You can make the body you like and add the*
> *face, like photoshop. But you should learn*
> *vfx if you want video*
> *But I want to use ai haha*
> *So you need to find the video, then add the face*

Christine sent me a link to a tutorial: 'best ever putin deepfake'.

Cathay was too busy to meet me after my Facebook interview. I ate a cold sandwich and returned to Cambridge. I missed clubbing, every night an opportunity for sex, for being passed between strangers like a bowling ball.

I squinted at my laptop. The screen was dusty. I could

not see where the logic began and ended.

Christine had left me her notes. She also helped me with my dissertation. I video called her one Saturday, and she was at the beach. Flushed clouds swam behind palm trees, fuzzy like peaches. She spun around, showed me the gleaming Pacific and her asymmetric swimming costume.

In the morning, I woke with a start, crying out for America. I went to the library. I worked on my dissertation. I drafted messages to Helen that I couldn't bring myself to send.

Helen had been an American visiting student at another college. She met Cathay at a 'Race Awareness in Classics' seminar. Helen, the start of her name a sigh. We slept together three times, the longest I'd spent in bed with anyone.

In the darkness of her warm room, I saw stars. It was the start of summer and the end of everything. She slipped through me, cut my lip, wet my thigh. Seeds poured from the poplar trees like smoke.

Cathay graduated and Helen went back to America, changing her cover photo on Facebook to a picture that my elbow was in. My fourth year, I felt along the inside of my cheek with my tongue, searching for her.

I applied for jobs. I passed the aptitude tests for most of the major tech companies, but I had nothing to talk about at interview.

It turned out that it was harder to move to America than I had anticipated.

Helen was at Yale now, finishing a PhD. We still messaged, every one or two years, as though only meeting by chance. Somehow, it was always me who sent the last message. I didn't know what the point of it was, except that it gave me a reason to live.

Helen asked after Cathay, who she had lost touch with. I told her that Cathay was, as always, very well.

Follow me . . . I wrote on Instagram, in promotion of my new OnlyFans account. Hashtagging, among other pleasures, *asiangirls*.

The technology was all there, open source and imperfect. I only needed to install the right dependencies, and find the words. Keiko appeared on the first attempt, arms folded and eyebrows filled in, smiling like she loved me. I dressed her in a red string bikini, against a whorl of grey. Dark hair licked the fullness of her breasts.

She knelt, head low and eyes wide, cheeks rosy. She parted her lips, but never widened her mouth. She was on all fours, peering over her shoulder. She wore lace-trimmed stockings, leather chokers and pleated skirts. I thought of the girls at school, who rolled up their skirts into belts. Letters were sent home, concerns for their safety. And I envied them. Those same girls all got conjunctivitis, from sharing mascara.

In the beginning, the responses to Keiko were not many. But they were embarrassingly sincere. I had done something that worked.

Someone did accuse me of working for the Chinese government, of trying to trick everyone into downloading spyware by making them think it was porn. *Nobody fall for this!!* But far fewer people, and I assumed they were people, were pissed off than I had expected. Hardly anyone seemed concerned that Keiko was so obviously fake.

Most of what was said to or about her meant nothing.

I picked from suggested captions and automated her DMs, deciding early on that I had nothing to say to anyone. She replied to every DM a randomised number of minutes under ten. One guy spoke to her all night, every night, before he lost interest. Two mirrors, bouncing light between them.

Who are you?
I am yours!

For a while I kept track of every interaction, followed the dribble of interest like a football score, like my home team were playing. I couldn't help myself. A piece of me had travelled somewhere I would never go.

No one cared when I cancelled my lunch-and-learns. I worked from home, exaggerating migraines, period pains, common colds. Winter came, flat and grey as steel. Simon drew my name for Secret Santa, and bought me everything on my online wish list. 'You must have been really good this year,' people in the office remarked, noticing how many presents I had.

Veronica returned to work in January with her hair in clumps, suddenly fat and pale. She announced that she was expecting a baby. Who would have a baby? Not Helen, who, despite having had mostly boyfriends, called straight people 'breeders'.

I missed her more than ever.

January dragged on. Interest in Keiko plateaued, and tailed off. Why this was, I would never know. Perhaps it was 'the algorithm'. I posted more regularly, which I had read that the algorithm liked. Keiko sank to the ground, her arms outstretched in supplication. Keiko pushed her overlarge breasts from side to side. Keiko displayed parts of herself that I had to manufacture on Photoshop.

Guys just aren't into desperate/needy girls.

At the same time, I was being punished for the shortcuts I had taken in the code. I would never be able to fix everything that was wrong with Keiko. There were bugs all over her, she was filthy. I spent a fortnight troubleshooting an integration that was working fine before, and talking to no one. My eyes dried out like petals, curling at the edges.

I often gave up, and was even taken offline a few times, for breach of conduct. But I couldn't stop myself from starting again, the way I always re-downloaded Instagram after I had deleted it. And I was relieved to find everything where I had left it. There was always some reward, something to be optimised, some rush.

A spurt of new subscribers. But it wasn't a stable income, yet. It would never be a stable income, possibly. Still, I resurrected my old fantasies of job offers from tech giants, and a feature in the *New Yorker* that Helen would see. 'The Asian fetish is a fantasy that exists apart from us, and we mustn't internalise,' I would say, looking hot for a Cambridge graduate, and naturally thin. 'And I have no qualms about taking money from those who objectify us.'

I imagined my beautiful, bewildered mother studying the pages of *Cosmopolitan* and guessing the meanings of keywords, and I wasn't sure how I felt.

My mother was a Communist beauty. She cut her own hair, and my father's. She wore men's jeans. I had been mortified by her when I was a child. It consoled me to think of Helen, approving of her jeans.

Helen would surely approve of Keiko. She herself once

had a profile on a sugar dating site. A New York college thing. She showed me the messages. *i don't usually do this kind of thing but you remind me of my ex wife.*

I laughed until it hurt.

Helen never actually had a sugar daddy, but an ex-boyfriend of hers, a 'wicked man', had bought her a ballgown that cost eleven hundred dollars. She slipped the straps off her shoulders and the dress pooled at our feet, molten silver. 'I've never felt comfortable naked,' she said. But perhaps she was only being ironic.

It turned out that Keiko was the name of the male orca from Iceland who had played Willy in *Free Willy*, a film I had never seen. Keiko had died of pneumonia, in the fjords of Norway, at the age of twenty-seven.

Meanwhile, the death threats. The rape threats. The mutilation threats. What the world would do to an Asian woman, and mean it as a compliment!

By the time Cathay and I met up for our belated Spring Festival celebration, it was actually spring.

A sudden burst of light had everyone in Central London wearing shorts and eating gelato, although it was nine degrees outside. Cathay had new curtain bangs, which she hadn't told me about. I didn't like that, although I had taken pleasure in telling her, before now, that I was too busy to meet up.

We ate at Cathay's dad's restaurant in Chinatown. The shift manager, Uncle Wei, refilled our glasses with white wine and baijiu. He checked over his shoulder for Uncle Eddie like a pantomime dame, as though we were still teenagers. He wouldn't leave us alone until we laughed and shushed him back.

'Thanks Uncle Wei,' we chorused.

It saddened me to think that he might be a pervert. The time I had spent in Keiko's world had made me more suspicious of perverts.

A large bead of wine dribbled down my chin.

I avoided the chicken feet that Cathay had ordered. The texture of the skin reminded me of scrotum. Cathay sucked on the bones defiantly, as though making a point about what a good Chinese girl she was.

I was reminded of the interviews she had given in publishing blogs, and retweeted. Repeating, like an incantation, 'I grew up in my dad's Chinese restaurant. I made drinks and waited tables. I was so ashamed.'

But hadn't my Cathay also studied classics at Cambridge? Hadn't she learned Latin and Ancient Greek at school?

I had tried to keep Keiko from her, but I couldn't help sending screenshots. I savoured her disbelief at the balance in my account, the increase in subscribers, how closely a message from a fan resembled something that someone had said to me in real life.

A little drunk, and undersocialised, sentences spilled from me like I was too small to contain them. Keiko's numbers had lurched suddenly forward, and I felt that I was on the cusp of something extraordinary. A great leap, and then another, and I might have enough money to quit my job. Another leap, and a name for myself, and job offers from all over.

I would buy a bigger house for my parents.

I would take Cathay on holiday.

Every bad thing, every humiliation I had endured over the course of my blessed life, would have been for something.

I drew breath, and realised that Cathay had not said any of what I had imagined.

'Are you all right?' I said.

She shrugged. 'I'm fine.'

She pinched a thread of morning glory between her chopsticks and put it in her mouth without looking at me.

'You're being quiet.'

'Well, I'm eating.'

I frowned, swirled vermicelli through the rice in my bowl. 'Do you still want to get bubble tea after this?'

'Sure. Why not.'

There were times, throughout the years, when I had wondered whether I was in love with Cathay. I imagined that it might have looked something like this, if I was.

We drained our glasses of wine and thimbles of baijiu. Uncle Wei lamented the dishes we hadn't finished. We assured him that we had enjoyed ourselves, and left the restaurant.

'Are you jealous?'

There, on the doorstep of Cathay's father's restaurant, I surprised myself by blurting out what I had already decided was true.

Cathay scoffed. 'Jealous of what?'

'My OnlyFans. My success.'

'Honestly, I'm not jealous at all.'

We walked on. Clearly, neither of us wanted bubble tea anymore. I studied the bright blue sky, obscured by red lanterns. I wondered what I could say to end this game of chicken, without losing.

'I find Uncle Wei kind of tragic,' I said. 'Don't you?'

'No.' Cathay paused. 'Actually, that's kind of problematic.'

I laughed. 'How?'

'The tragic Chinese man.' Cathay made quotes in the air with her fingers. 'Obviously, that's problematic.'

'But I never called him a "tragic Chinese man".' I copied her fingers, guns twitching in the air. 'He's just a Chinese man, who I find tragic.'

I stopped walking. 'I know you do too,' I insisted.

'You don't know what I think.'

'I think you're jealous of me.'

I laughed. But the laughter died in my mouth, betraying what we both knew: that I had never been more serious.

Cathay folded her arms. Solemn, like a priestess. Her eyes were dark crystals. Her new curtain bangs framed her face like a hood.

'I don't feel like getting bubble tea anymore. I think I'll just go home.'

She started walking, and I followed.

'Why don't you just tell me how you're feeling?'

The words felt familiar. Perhaps I had heard them on a show.

We turned onto Newport Place. I forgot that they had demolished the pagoda years ago, and I felt suddenly displaced. But there was the car park. There was the Hong Kong-style bakery, crowded, like everywhere else, by students from the mainland.

'Why don't I tell you how I'm feeling?' It was Cathay's

turn to stop. She gave a small, mean laugh. 'I fucking hate your OnlyFans.'

I couldn't believe her.

'It's true,' she continued. 'I hate it. It's fucking degrading and disgusting and depressing. I don't know how you can stand it.'

'Oh come on.'

'All you're doing is giving all these men with Asian fetishes exactly what they want. You're feeding the part of them that gets off on Asian women being small and meek and submissive. You're confirming everything they believe about us.'

'They'd be like that with or without me. With or without Keiko. I might as well take money off them.'

I remembered, and rolled my eyes. 'She's not even real,' I added.

'But these men are. These are real men. The screenshots you sent me of what they've been saying have literally kept me up at night.'

'I thought you'd laugh. Because it's all ridiculous. And honestly, I thought you would be more open-minded about this, more sex-positive.'

'Laugh?' Cathay did laugh. 'You can't just disappear for three months because you're obsessed with getting famous on OnlyFans and expect me not to worry about you. I've tried to be open-minded. But every time I've tried to talk to you properly, you've dismissed me. And the screenshots you sent honestly triggered me.'

She narrowed her eyes.

'And I know they would have triggered you.'

There was a white guy filming us! I opened my mouth

indignantly, but I couldn't make any sound come out. It was just as well. He was only taking a selfie, with all the lanterns. He flipped the phone and showed his friends.

'You know, there've been times recently when I really needed you?'

Cathay's lip wobbled, and I almost believed her.

'Like when?'

'David messaged me. He wants to meet up.'

I snorted. 'So that's what this is about? Fucking David? And you have the audacity to lecture me about indulging white men?'

Cathay's cheeks were bright pink. Was it the wine, or had I succeeded in humiliating her?

'For the first time in my life, I'm actually doing something for me.' I swallowed the twitch of guilt, watched the lanterns as they swayed. 'I'm not like you. My parents have sacrificed so much for me.'

'My parents have sacrificed so much for me!' Cathay shrieked, startling us both.

I grimaced. 'I know. I just meant – your dad is British born.'

'Oh my God.'

'He's more understanding. And he's so proud of you, for like, existing. Both your parents are. You know how jealous of you I was at Cambridge? I'd never met a Chinese person before who just did whatever they wanted.'

It hurt to look at Cathay directly, like the sun.

Obviously, I knew she didn't just do whatever she wanted.

'We were eighteen, at Cambridge,' she said. 'Now we're nearly fucking thirty. When are you going to stop making excuses? Grow up, people do it all the time. Get a new job, if you hate yours. Go on a date.'

'I can't go on a date, I'm in love with Helen.'

Cathay's eyebrows, filled in with grey powder, shot up. '*My* Helen?'

People passed, Chinese people.

My face was hot. My fingers, balled into fists, were cold.

'Oh my God.' Cathay shook her head, her John Lennon-style glasses trembling on the bridge of her nose. 'You think you're an adult now because you have OnlyFans? You're a child! You're a child with fucking *Neopets*!'

I marched away from Cathay, remembering, among other crimes, the 'cool data' book she had bought me for my last birthday.

She was right about me in other ways, of course.

And I was wrong about Keiko. Because she was real. I saw her, crossing the Covent Garden piazza like a shadow. A woman who looked enough like Keiko that I felt awkward about having seen her naked, and the things that I had done to her. She looked less Japanese than usual. She wore a long, camel-coloured coat, and drank taro-flavoured bubble tea.

I wanted to take a picture with her, but I didn't know how to ask. So I followed her. And I would follow her until I could get Cathay to come and see for herself, and know what I was talking about.

Heroes of the South West

Ali Roberts

Conner mouths *indignity*, careful not to trip over the syllables. 'Suffer the indignity,' he says. 'I've had to suffer the indignity of –'

A car passes; not his dad's. He knows his dad's car: two of the wheels are black. The spare ones like you get from under the floor in the boot. Also, on what his dad told him is the *wheel arch*, there's a big beige smear of unpainted primer or something.

His dad's car's a *jalopy*? Best not risk it. Once, when he'd said *clandestine* at the British Folk Craft Museum, his sister Megan said he was '*clan-destined* to die alone', and high-fived their dad who almost doubled over, cackling.

'Suffer the *indignity* of being –' *Denied entry* doesn't sound climactic. *Banished*? Possibly *ejected*. 'From my writing workshop due to unpaid –' It's not even expensive. Megan (fifteen) got a new computer on her last birthday; Conner (sixteen) got a wallet.

'Ejected from my writing workshop because you're –' There must be a more emotive word than *cheap*.

His dad had given him this wallet like: 'Here you go,

son.' He'd actually called Conner 'son' like they were in some soppy film where we cut to fifteen years later: it's Conner's wedding day; Conner looks across the chapel and takes out the same well-worn wallet. He smiles at his father; a single tear rolls off his cheek onto the wallet, dampening a patch of pleather as violins swell.

'It's real leather,' his dad had told him when Conner unwrapped it.

Jan sees his son from the footpath at the bottom of the hill and waves. No wave back, so he shrugs at Conner and carries on walking towards him. The car, which he reversed into a ditch this morning, is now at T. C. Motors with a cracked back axle. 'Repair on that'll be more than the whole thing's worth,' is what the mechanic said.

Jan shouts, 'You're out early, Con?'

Apologies for last night. First, taking the piss out of the cowboy hat. Son's wardrobe: not Jan's choice, or concern. Second, knocking over his 'totems' or whatever he calls them. They're not that weird. Claire has Conner's and Megan's baby teeth set in resin on her keyring, that's kind of the same. Third, sorry for calling you two kids little f-word c-words and threatening to leave forever.

This should in turn prompt a reciprocal apology of: 'Dad, sorry for being a nightmare and generally ungrateful; sorry not just for losing my phone but for lying about it; sorry, also, for repeatedly calling my little sister things like *harlot* and *languisher*.'

Maybe, later, at home, a bonus joint apology with Megan, possibly in chorus: 'Dad, we understand x or y is hard for you at the moment especially with Mum working nights. Sorry, also, for criticising the dinner(s).' Something like that.

'Where's the car?' Conner says when Jan gets up close.

'Head gasket blew,' Jan lies, exhaling, resisting the impulse to match Conner's tone. It's what Jan lands on to defer his responsibility. He does another shrug, confident Conner won't bother asking what a head gasket is. 'Inevitable, really,' he says, pressing the point that it is the car, not him, who is at fault here.

Conner nods as if he's dealt with a few blown head gaskets in his time.

'Con, I've had a call and I got an interview at a place down by the harbour. It's in about an hour.'

'So, are we getting a taxi?'

'You paying?' Jan says, laughing. Then he catches Conner's *for fuck's sake* eyeroll and says, 'I thought we'd get the number nine. It's only along the Greenway and down the hill.'

Reacting to the imperious stance – pristine boot bag in one extended hand, portfolio of severe charcoal drawings in the other – Jan goes, 'Well then, pardner, s'posin' I piggyback yuh? Saddle up, Rawhide.'

Conner and his dad take the number nine along the Greenway in silence.

Since Conner started wearing the fedora, Megan and his dad have been: Rawhide, Rawhide, Rawhide; giving each other shit-eating looks across the table when Conner wears it at dinner; shouting little yee-haws, whirling phantom lassos.

'You look the spit of him in your new hat!' Megan

squawked the first time the Rawhide Healthydog Interdental Chew Treat advert came on the telly: a helpless-looking, curly-haired little boy wearing tasselled chaps gets bucked off a Labrador he's been straddling like it's a horse then the Labrador gives his face a lick like it's all better and they're friends again.

'You've got to admit it, Con. Exactly the same,' his dad said. And there'd been no Mum to step in because she'd already started on the night shifts.

They're *infantilising* him. He whispers the word to himself a couple of times, 'In-fan-til-i-sing,' down the aisle of the bus, away from his dad.

Last night Conner took off his hat and put it beside them on the table. First he apologised, *solemnly*, for losing his phone, then he tried to ask about borrowing that sixty quid, not mentioning it was for the writing classes his dad had promised to pay for.

'Boy howdy,' his dad said, nudging Megan, 'you best get yourself a job, cowpoke.'

They both roared laughing again, a pale scrim of potato matter covering their ~~spasming~~ *shuddering tongues*, Conner wrote in his journal before bed. He'd looked up synonyms for *spasm*. Also the word *scrim* which he liked the sound of, and the meaning turned out to be close to what he was looking for.

'He won't get a job, Dad, he's too into his *alone time*,' Megan said, mime-wanking, eyebrow raised, as if mere seconds away from saying she'd once walked in when Conner forgot to lock the door during his bath.

Conner felt humiliated, no, *demeaned*, and had to bite his lips together to keep from gobbing his mouthful of oven chips in Megan's face.

Conner shifts in his bus seat to get out his journal.

> *The Greenway. A tunnel of trees. From Bickswell Academy to the sea. A dark vein in the tree of my life?* [mixed metaphor?]
> *The aorta* [look up definition] *pumping the blood to the surface of my grievanced heart.* [grievanced = made-up word?]

Jan spends most of the bus journey trying to spit-shine a scuff off his toecap, eventually realising it's where the steel's worn through.

Conner's staring, mouthing things, scribbling in his little book.

This wearing a weird hat thing, Jan suspects – although it's none of his business – is something Conner's picked up off the internet, probably. Some kind of trend from those bigoted message boards he's seen on the telly? Like a signal: this cheap knock-off hat I got off my skiving bullshit artist of an uncle means x or y thing about – hopefully not – men's rights or race politics. He's too soft for that. But just soft enough to be moulded? Maybe.

Every time Conner comes back from visiting his shithead uncle he's got some new idea. 'One day I want to live on a houseboat like Uncle Deano.'

Uncle Deano *has* to live on a houseboat because he's a layabout who sold his ex-wife's car for ketamine. The land doesn't want him.

Jan turns to Conner. The bus is silent so, without making eye contact, he whispers, 'Con, I'm sorry for taking the piss out of your hat. Your *fedora*?'

'OK,' Conner says.

Conner's working up to saying something about the money for the writing workshop but his dad gives him a miserable look again, like when he said the thing about the head casket.

Last night, when Conner's dad came to his room to tell him dinner was nearly ready, Conner told him about his phone being nicked. 'One of the Lethaby boys,' he'd said, 'the one who's expelled, he hangs about at the gates –'

'And you just *let* him take it?' his dad cut in. Then both of them went silent for a bit, his dad just looking Conner up and down like, *I can see why*; like, *I'd have took it off you and all*.

'I lost it,' Conner said to make all the horrible looking at him stop.

'What?' His dad got up, gripping the sides of his hair.

At least this way he'd only be irresponsible. 'I lost it.'

'Me and your mum pay your contract. You careless, ungrateful –'

With each word he beat his fist on Conner's desk and Conner accidentally *exclaimed*? – too old-fashioned – maybe *blurted*, 'My totems!' as all his precariously balanced curiosities clattered to the desktop.

'Totems, Conner?' his dad said. Giving Conner another shame-filled look, he prodded the last one standing – the one made of horsehair-tangled barbed wire wrapped round a pencil – and the crow's skull tumbled off the top.

Conner spent the rest of the bit between hometime and dinnertime gluing his totems together, sorting them out of the collapsed pile: driftwood-spiked-through-with-biro goes with rook skull; wheat-stem-woven-around-mechanical-pencil goes with raven.

The bus chokes into a higher gear.

Conner tries it: 'Dad, d'you think I could borrow that sixty quid?'

'What for?'

What for? To honour a promise is what for. 'Coat?'

'Hardly the time, Con,' he says, brushing the lapel of his too-big, navy-blue interview blazer.

Jan says, again, quieter, 'Hardly the time.'

One: Jan's *literally* just told Conner (admittedly a semi-truth) about the car. Two: Conner's lost his phone and although last night's grilling may've been too harsh – especially because Claire's paying not only Conner's but also Jan's phone bill at the moment – this signals generally careless behaviour undeserving of any reward. Three: from where? What sixty quid? The whole family, extended family – even cousins he hasn't spoken to in years – know about him getting sacked from Swann's.

Ten years working up from oiling bolts and pressure-washing tractor tyres to become a surveyor.

For purposes of the CV: Enthusiastically and professionally led a whole (admittedly small) team of talented agricultural engineers (mechanics); with rapidity and excellent results, performed (enough) rigorous mechanical tests (to give Jan early-onset arthritis) according to strict UK guidelines.

And they sack him for eating his lunch down the Jackdaw.

At least three of the empties on the table weren't his. Try telling that to the pack of pale-faced bastards who've installed the diagnostic scanner that'll oust you. Now everyone second-guesses including him in a round as if he's got a habit. Shameful way to let a person go.

The bus turns, heading down the hill into Widcombe. Conner takes out a book as thick as a breeze block that's got loads of bits of folded paper and sticky notes stuffed in it.

Grimoire: The Collected Tales of P. B. MacNaughton.

'Christ. They making you read that thing in school?' Jan says.

Jan gets a look from Conner: eyes half closed, head cocked back a bit. It's a look Jan's learned to read. It says, *Philistine.*

Jan's only read an aspirational travelogue about scuba diving, the biography of the Mars landing astronaut bloke who disappeared mysteriously, and the half-dozen frenzied pamphlets the Anglican Farmers Union have put through their letterbox.

'No. I just like reading,' Conner says.

'OK, professor.'

Conner holds the book open but doesn't read.

He's been using *Grimoire* as a kind of writing workshop file. Someone's printout of his latest piece falls onto his lap and he shoves it in the back. Unable to unfold it since last week, he's left their criticisms unread.

He'd been asked to introduce this story at last week's writing workshop. 'The Goatherd's Drum' is one of a projected series of tales entitled *The Travails of Dumnon Meriadoc*. 'Dumnon, the protagonist, is a brave – though flawed – adventurer, in the Dark Age South West,' he'd said, 'in the style of P. B. MacNaughton's heroes,' and this girl, Hailey, interrupted like, 'P. B. MacNaughton is a chauvinist. Violence against women, etc. etc.,' and Mr Pearson just let her carry on, even though she'd cut Conner off in the middle of a sentence. Then Hailey looked over at pretentious Caleb who sat there nodding with his eyes closed.

Caleb always goes on about French books and smokes cigarettes because the authors are smoking on the book covers. Conner smokes because he wants to and he's pretty much gotten used to the taste.

Conner, stumbling, had tried to reclaim MacNaughton, grasping as if a blanket had been pulled off his flabby naked chest. MacNaughton's plots, his imagination, his language – most of all his *language*.

'How often are his vile antagonists described as "swarthy"?' Pretentious Caleb asked the room. Admittedly unaware of the meaning of that word but assuming it is often used in bad taste, Conner stayed quiet. He could, however, think of at least three instances off the top of his head.

'Stop's coming up.' His dad nudges him and Conner snaps *Grimoire* closed, fumbling, suddenly anxious, trying to catch it so his writing doesn't fall out or, worse, it could open on the back flap – about the author – where MacNaughton grins out from the darkness beneath the brim of his fedora.

Jan hops off the bus – spry, confident, vigorous – and strides down the promenade waving Conner to follow, recounting the phases from that *How to Ace Your Job Interview* video Claire sent him.

Handshake first: not too firm – typical mistake. Too firm and they'll think you're overasserting your dominance, challenging them somehow.

Also, be sure to have dry hands. Jan rubs his hands on the inside of his blazer pockets.

They'll ask something general: 'So, Jan, tell me about yourself.'

This is not an opportunity to share your hobbies, it's an elevator pitch. Don't say too much. Experience, skillset, mindset. Eye contact. Don't draw attention to the blazer; it's old and too big.

'Why *this* job, Jan?'

He'll say something about the company: the tourism industry is great for the county's economy. And the *ecology*: mention the money they give to the Widcombe Biome Trust which conserves the cliff-nesting bird population. Lastly, the cutting-edge hydrofoil boats. He'll ask how many knots you do in one of those things. Then he'll link the boats back to his agricultural engineering background to tie a bow on it.

'Well, you'll mostly be taking care of things over at the gift shop.'

Of course, yes. Jan'll tell them he can also do basic maths and stand still for a really long time.

'So, what makes *you* the right person for the job, Jan?'

Well, for one, to be able to answer the question, 'What do you do?' with something approaching the truth. Also, a deeply felt but not exactly progressive feeling that a job tangentially involving big futuristic boats is just more *proper* to him than something important but emasculating like Claire's job at the care home. 'We always need carers,' she'd said.

He'll call himself a *salesman* rather than a *retail assistant*. 'I'm a salesman down at Widcombe Hydrofoil,' he'll say, and chuck back half the pint he's just been bought, ready to field everyone's questions about hydrodynamic hull technologies.

Conner looks around the harbour: ice cream shop, Cap'n Zach's Pasty Shack, ice cream shop.

'Where's the interview?'

His dad points: the gift shop attached to the place that does the hydrofoil tours out round the point to see the last of the terns that nest in the cliffs. It's at the end of the pier where the posh boats are moored. Big white ones called things like *Evangeline*, *Calliope* and *Glory Days*.

The tide's high and Conner looks in the polished side of *Calliope* which curves out above him. Red-faced, pudgy. More so because of the angle but definitely filling out. *Gy-nae-co-mas-ti-a*. He turns it over in his head, this word Megan had once pointedly mentioned after learning it in a PSHE sexual health lesson. 'It means little boy breasts disease,' she'd said, 'and you get it when you spend too much time tugging on your knob.' *Gynaecomastia*, noun: that which leads one to stand, near-sobbing, before the mirrored bathroom cabinet, post-shower towel wrapped about your waist, pinching and kneading your chubby and hairless chest.

'Conner,' his dad calls from the gift shop entrance, 'come wait in here, they've got chairs.'

'I'll stay here.'

Jan, through clenched teeth, goes, 'No, please wait in here for me.'

Idea is: keep him close, keep some eyes on him. Even the dozy, jaded eyes of a harbourside retail assistant. Trust him? Alone? Near rich people's property? Nope.

The first and last time Jan and Claire trusted Conner to babysit Megan, he told her the artist that lives in the big house at the top of their hill – the one who makes those tacky sailboat espresso mugs – once roasted a young girl in his pottery kiln and ground her up for dog food. Megan pretended to be ill and missed almost a week of school.

Jan's said it before and he says it again now: 'If you can't be responsible in your own home, how can I trust you here?'

No movement from Conner so Jan goes for a forced sympathetic grimace, palms out like sad Jesus revealing stigmata.

When that fails as well he crosses the pier, hooks Conner's arm and marches him into the gift shop. On the way he checks his reflection in the side of a boat named *Evangeline*. The concave hull squats him flat like he's been thumbed into the concrete.

Conner sits and reads *Grimoire* by the manager's office door across from a ginger girl around his age who's flicking the corner of her CV.

His dad, after being told he was far too early, has gone to 'familiarise himself with the stock'.

She's watching him, this girl. Watching the book,

maybe? Conner ignores her until she says, 'What are you *reading*?'

Normally he'd smirk, pull the book up to his face so she could see the whole cover, but today he flattens it against his legs, waiting until she leaves or looks away so it doesn't seem like she's the reason he's slipping the dust jacket into his satchel.

This edition of *Grimoire* often elicits that kind of repulsion; it's half the reason Conner bought it. The cover is intended to look as if it's bound in the skin – a *pelt*? – cut from the midriff of a flayed mermaid, below and including the navel, where the turquoise scales fade to greyish human flesh.

If she'd been genuinely interested; if she, or anyone, decided to ask, 'What are you reading?' without a tone suggesting a *the fuck* between the *what* and the *are*, he'd be more than willing to explain: the jacket is in fact a reference to MacNaughton's most famous tale, 'Thunder in the Upper Deep', in which a group of sailors hunt for an island that's home to cannibal mermaids, only to become stranded there, eventually turning cannibal themselves and hunting said mermaids for food.

Somewhere in his peripheral vision Conner's dad is weighing Widcombe Hydrofoil Souvenir mugs in his palms, spinning old-fashioned postcard racks.

Conner skips to the back of *Grimoire* and reads one of the more realist stories he's been avoiding. 'Seed of Cain' is about a bare-knuckle boxer, a huge man with spade-like hands who descends into madness, eventually murdering his wife on their wedding night.

It's short and brutal. Conner feels a discomfort that

he's been resisting. Possibly it's the real-life parallel: MacNaughton's author bio notes he was once a bare-knuckle boxer. More likely it's the narrator's dwelling too long on the final image of the unconscious bride's shattered teeth.

Jan's holding a Scenic Scenes fridge magnet. It's got a tiny LCD screen that scrolls through videos of apparently local things that Jan's never seen, taking place on brighter, more brilliant days than he's ever experienced: an otter bounding out of a stream into the arms of a little girl; a group of teens cliff-diving into a crystal lagoon; a family in hairnets cutting fudge into cubes with a bit of taut wire.

The hydrofoil tour boat zips into the harbour. A parade of grockles streams off. Men in puce trousers; women in flowing white shirts. They potter about at an ice cream kiosk, buy nothing, and amble back up the main drag to the restaurants.

Conner would tell anyone who'd ask that his favourite MacNaughton story is 'Their Name Was Darkness'. It's about this moorland shepherd who, 'upon peering through the boughs of wind-bent blackthorns', sees 'primeval figures, stalking through the Stygian dark, preying on his flock' and he wards them off by filling his paddock with totems made from blackthorn limbs and sheep skulls.

MacNaughton has a lot to say about fear. Conner rehearses this argument in his head, although it's disturbed by 'Seed of Cain''s flashes of blood on lace. 'To combat the darkness, you must first accept it, then imprint upon it your desire,' the shepherd tells his son. That's why the skulls at the top of their totems are filled with pieces of silver. Conner's own are made of the skulls of carrion birds that used to peck his eyes out in nightmares – all picked off the roadside with held breath, bleached, and stuck on little poles made of found materials wound around, or pierced with, writing implements.

Jan goes to sit by Conner because, one: he'll be able to pass off his embarrassing nervous energy as sincere but faltering father-son discussion and, two: if he apologises now, Conner might return the thumbs-up Jan's planning to give him when he enters the interview room. Maybe even a good luck, 'Good luck, Dad.'

'Conner.'

'Huh?'

Already not ideal. Jan tries anyway: 'Conner, I wanted to apologise.'

'Again? Now?' he says.

'Yes, now. Why? What's wrong with now? Christ.'

Jan's prospective colleague is there in front of them, slouched behind the POS system in tiny white shorts with a little pubey moustache. Summer job, probably. Off to university in a few months after he's taught Jan to recite by rote the contents of the silver and gold tour packages and their attendant free-beverage benefits.

It takes a minute to notice he's being addressed by this boy because Jan's busy deciphering the slogan beneath the logo on his little blue-peaked cap. *Adventure Awaits*.

Conner kicks his foot.

'Yan Wyburn?' the boy says.

'It's Jan – Jan like John, with a hard J – I'm Jan

Wyburn, yes.'

'Manager's ready for you.'

Jan looks back at Conner whose nose remains stuffed in the ass crack of that massive pompous book. Entering the office, Jan grips the silky innards of his blazer pockets before offering his hand for a shake.

'Yan, nice to meet you,' the woman, as yet unborn on the date of Jan's last job interview, says. 'Take a seat.'

Jan sits.

'It didn't say your age on your CV.'

'Should it?'

'No, no, that's fine, I was just wondering. You're aware this is a weekend position?'

'I am aware of that, yes.'

'What a lovely accent,' she says. 'Where are you from, originally?'

'Here.'

Conner, alone apart from the till operator, gets out his journal and perches near the window.

Black water reflects the houses' gables [check if 'gables' correct] *like netherworld mountain ranges*, he writes, *and sketchy fronds of liver-coloured weed hang in drips like clotting blood from the walkways' undercarriages*. He underlines this sentence, puts a big ring around it, and a tick next to it. *A blanket of foam laps at the* – the bit where the boats are pulled up – *the runway*?

Grimoire falls off Conner's lap along with the reams of loose paper he's been keeping stuffed between its pages. The top one is an annotated printout of 'The Goatherd's Drum':

> *Dumnon walked towards the meander in the stream where a hermit kept goats* [great first line]. *It was ~~agonisingly~~ hot in the valley and a haze rose ~~sullenly~~ off the quagmire*[?]. [too many adverbs here? Confused? Consider revising/removing]

It's Hailey's printout. She's put a question mark next to *quagmire* but no explanation of what she was questioning.

On the back, below the final paragraph, in green pen: 'Does little girl' – she's referring to the child who Dumnon, hypnotised by the goatherd's drumbeat, drowns in the bog – 'Does little girl need to die? Could D not find a way to overcome hypnosis? Better for character development? More complex?'

Hailey had said the same during the workshop and Conner responded, 'But, the brutality, that's kind of the point,' although he wasn't sure it was and, truthfully, Conner finds endings difficult, often impossible.

She's signed off with, 'I like it. You're talented – H.'

'Conner?' someone says behind him, shocking him out of his reverie.

Conner spins round. It's Pretentious Caleb.

'I could tell by the fucking hat. Where were you today?'

So nobody in writing class knew. Mr Pearson hadn't said anything. Conner shrugs.

Caleb's standing in front of Conner, crotch near face height.

Conner's mum vaguely knows Pretentious Caleb so when those two stop in the street to speak to each other, Conner nods shyly to Caleb who stands there, just like this, with his hands on his hips. Someone so tall with such good posture has clearly never had to endure anything.

Caleb is sexual in a way that makes Conner feel as if he's being interrogated. He talks about sex in literature in a knowing way, the *intimacy* of this, the *eroticism* of that. He's probably fucked a lot. He's probably convinced poor Hailey to fuck him.

'So, are you going for this job as well?' Caleb's nose wrinkles in disbelief.

'Fuck no,' Conner says.

Caleb's thrown, stutters a bit, his stance shifts, then he sits down opposite Conner. 'I know, right,' he says. 'Such an inane job.'

Caleb looks smaller now, sitting down with his toes turned inward.

Over Caleb's shoulder, the till operator sighs as his pyramid of Heroes of the South West playing cards collapses. They're the same cards Conner's parents used to play sevens with after dinner: backs printed with moustachioed blokes, mostly called Francis, standing, chins raised, in front of rippling sails and slate cliffs, sometimes wearing ruffs or pith helmets.

'Well what are you doing in here, then?' Caleb says, looking at his hands, not at Conner.

'Waiting for my dad.' Conner jerks his head towards the manager's office door.

'Your *dad*'s going for this job?' Caleb says. He laughs but it's a thin laugh.

Conner doesn't take his eyes off Caleb until he's watched the laughter die on the end of his tongue.

When Conner mentioned Pretentious Caleb once, his

dad said it was jealousy, said, 'Careful with that word "pretentious", Con. He's only pretentious if he doesn't actually believe what he's saying.'

Conner now sees he's vindicated. The forced aloofness with which Caleb scans the room, scowling at a window fitting or ceiling tile, only serves to thin his bogus skin, under which Conner can see a roiling nausea of embarrassment and anxiety. Sitting here, unprepared to recite the biographies and potted analyses of cigarette-smoking philoso-novelists like some lazy incantation, he looks twitchy, skittish.

Conner's dad may be desperate but Caleb's desperation goes a layer deeper. Caleb, like Conner, is desperate not to seem desperate. It's like looking into a mirror, albeit one that'll make you taller and more handsome. Conner takes off his fedora and folds it into his satchel with the *Grimoire* dust jacket.

Jan spends the bus ride home on the phone to Claire who consoles him.

He becomes bitter and complains. He's the wrong demographic, the woman had suggested; he was perhaps *overqualified* for the position, she'd said. Claire tells him off: 'You're better than this,' she says.

Jan says, 'Exactly! I know! That's what Conner said as well.' Conner hadn't said that, but a complex exchange of gestures post-interview had communicated something similar.

Claire says, 'The whining, Jan, not the job.' Then she tells him chin up because she has to leave for work. 'There's chilli in the slow cooker,' she says.

Meanwhile Conner, hatless, frantically scribbles in his book.

'Con,' Jan says.

Conner pokes a full stop at the end of his line and looks up at Jan.

'Did you know that boy in the gift shop?' Jan says.

'Caleb, from writing class.'

Writing class. *That* sixty quid. Jan's heart drops into his bowels. Pretending he's always remembered, Jan nods slowly and slyly pats his pockets for his wallet.

Pointing at the page left open on Conner's lap, Jan says, 'That for class?'

Jan shifts closer and for once Conner doesn't close the journal. He's written and underlined *Goatherd's Drum – New Ending* at the top of the page.

> *Dumnon grits his teeth against the hypnotic thumping. He blinks hard and suddenly it's as if the rains have stopped falling from the clouds inside his head. He releases the little girl's neck. Her limbs slap against the wet surface of the bog and she lies still, wheezing.*
>
> *The goatherd beats his drum quicker and Dumnon stumbles towards him now, through the knee-deep stream. His eyes feel crossed, as if his brain has been halved and each half is fighting against the other.*
>
> *The drum pounds, dumb and frenzied, as Dumnon grasps for the goatherd's neck. His grip tightens and the goatskin hood falls to reveal the man's red, terrified face.*

Dumnon squeezes, staring into the goatherd's bulging eyes, and a shaft of sunlight, like an eye of God, pierces the clouds in his mind. As his vision returns he sees his own broad silhouette shimmer like a ghost in the choking man's pupils.

As long as this goatherd lives, so will that shadow of Dumnon in his tear-filled eye. If he dies, another will beat his drum.

Dumnon releases the goatherd's neck and strikes through the skin of the drum with a stone.

After he heaves its hollow barrel into the stream the frenzied goats come to rest, lying in loose circles and grazing along the riverbank. Dumnon crouches to wipe his face with a dew-wetted palm.

The little girl has regained her breath and is watching Dumnon from under a tree. Afraid, caked in muck, but alive.

Glue

Danny Beusch

As the lift descends, Emma rations. If she has just six a day, every day, then how long is left? A year at most, she thinks, leaving the office, her shadow long in the winter sun. She crosses the road, ducks around a corner, looks left and right and over her shoulder before slipping off her heels and swapping them for a pair of trainers. Glancing at her watch, she curses the hordes of Christmas shoppers.

When she first saw the advertisement, the date and time, Emma opened her calendar and cleared the afternoon. I apologise for any inconvenience caused, she wrote in each of the emails, but a business-critical situation has arisen that demands my urgent attention. The FTSE 100 tech company she had harassed for a meeting did not reply.

Darting through the crowds, Emma feels light-headed. Sweat prickles her lower back. She missed breakfast, lunch too, but this is the usual way; she has never eaten her fill. Her narrow frame, her jutting collarbone – as Emma was growing up, they drove her mother mad, even though the GP kept saying that children are fussy, that Emma would eat if hungry.

In the kitchen in university halls, the other girls used to stare at Emma while she struggled through a spoonful of bolognese, or a handful of chips, sharing eyerolls and knowing looks. Now, she leans into her accents and angles, accentuating them with catwalk cuts and shades of black. She is precise, a surgeon's scalpel; the partners at the law firm lap it up. But today, when she holds out her arm, she feels it shake, sees her fingers tremble. Focus, she tells herself.

The lack of control makes her nauseous. She reaches into her handbag, finds the yellow wallet, flicks through its compartments until she reaches 1989. Inside, there is a book of ten first class stamps bought off eBay. She eases apart the perforations, covers her mouth with one hand as if she is about to cough. With her other hand, she pops the stamp onto the tip of her tongue, remembers her first time.

She was six years old, watching her mum sign a tower of Christmas cards. You have an important job, sweetheart, her mum said. You are in charge of envelopes. A teacher, before marrying a banker, her manner was exaggerated and she demonstrated the licking of a stamp like a dog lapping at water. Pop it in the top-right corner, straight as you can.

Between them was a tin from which Emma's mum rewarded herself after every five cards. Caramel Cups, Raspberry Revelations, Strawberry Surprises, Toffee Chews. Each elicited a mischievous grin, a sharp intake of breath. Go on, she said to Emma, holding out the tin with imploring eyes. To keep your strength up.

No thanks, Mama.

Emma did not understand the appeal: everything tasted the same; everything tasted of nothing. She picked up the stamps, inched one apart. Between thumb and forefinger, she brought it to her mouth, licked the underside.

Her tastebuds buzzed. Her tongue jolted back. Her stomach growled. Her mouth flooded with saliva.

Sweetheart, are you paying attention?

Emma ignored the irritation in her mum's voice, swallowed down the spittle, licked again. Her mouth tingled. Hot, sweet waves cascaded down her throat, warmed her belly. She looked to the tin of chocolates, the garish, crinkly wrappers, the way the colours of the rainbow blurred and danced in the light. The saturated stamp fell apart in her fingers.

Emma! her mum said. Do you actually want to help?

Feeling steady again, head clear, Emma removes the stamp and drops it into the nearest bin, on top of the disposable coffee cups and McDonald's wrappers. She checks her watch, speeds up. Her tongue sings, a hymn, a symphony of flavour.

Leaving Bond Street Tube station, Emma loads the webpage on her phone: Icons of Britain, an auction at Sotheby's. She double- and triple-checks the time, the order of proceedings. It is the final lot she must wait for, that she craves, even though it is out of her price range: a block of four Penny Blacks, mint condition, from the rarest printing plate. They are her favourites, the way they linger on her tongue, coat her mouth, for hours. Perhaps it is their age, the time the flavours have had to mature.

The other directors are into wine; at meetings, over drinks, they boast of hundreds, thousands, splurged on dusty bottles abandoned to their dank, dark cellars. Not

Emma, who searches eBay, Oxfam, Apfelbaum night after night for stamps. Never self-adhesive, or barcoded – which are no different than licking an envelope – Emma buys old, buys vintage. It is not cheap, but her salary and ever-growing bonus finally allow her this. She cannot believe how much of her life has been spent waiting.

When you're older, her mum had said, every time Emma asked if she could start receiving pocket money like all the others in her class. When you eat your dinner. When I know you won't spend it on anything stupid. When I know you're out of that phase.

She caved when Emma was ten and passed over a pound, holding her with a lingering look that said don't you even dare.

The corner shop was two streets away, a well-trodden journey with no roads to cross. Emma ran all the way, coin tight in her palm, and asked the woman behind the counter if they sold stamps.

No singles, my love. Book of eight second class is £1.92.

Emma stared at her lonely coin, blinked away tears. She took a paper bag, part-filled it with the bulkiest pick and mix, stashed the twenty pence change inside her coat pocket, zipping it all the way up, double-checking for gaps. Back home, watching TV with her mum, Emma made a show of chewing, of working clumps from her molars with tongue and fingernails, of giddy, sugar-high giggling, even though her gums ached and the sweets were a gooey mass of nothingness.

The waiting, the hunger, the deception, the secrecy; Emma has started to think of those times more often. On the first day when she couldn't find a Penny Black for sale, she assumed it was a mistake: a network error, a browser issue, a failure to refresh cookies. But the next day was the same, and the day after that. And now it has been over six months. She has spoken to collectors and dealers, sent messages on Facebook, scoured Reddit posts, attended fairs up and down the country. She has not managed to track down a single Penny Black, until this auction, with its reserve price of £400,000: more than triple what the lot would have fetched a year ago. There are other favourites – James and the Giant Peach, one of ten from a Roald Dahl special edition set – that have vanished from sale too.

Something has rocked the market. Today, Emma will find out what it is.

The shoppers keep coming, hurtling towards her, as Emma darts around them, onto the road and back again, their bags crashing against her thigh. It is the couples that frustrate her the most, the way their fingers stick together, even when the rest of their bodies are a metre apart.

Is she jealous, craving the feel of another's hand in hers? She shakes the thought. It's been decades since Emma has had an urge, an inclination, for all that. Being alone suits her, gives her the freedom she needs, that she never had at home or at school or at uni. Besides, where would she find someone, someone like her? And what would they taste like?

Emma's first and only kiss was around the back of the mobile classrooms, aged fifteen. I love skinny girls, Jonathan Rodgers said, moments before lurching towards her. She didn't like the way his hair fell in curtains, the way his smile was more like a sneer, but she had grown impatient for change. She assumed he would taste of nothing, but as his tongue pushed into her mouth, writhed against hers, the sourness was overwhelming and she gagged. Up crept his hand, edging across her protruding ribs and towards her barely there breast; she tried to turn away but his grip on the back of her head was clamp-like. And so, two hands on his chest, she pushed him.

Are you frigid or something? he said, wiping his mouth, his red flaky lips. You know, I only did this for a dare.

Just the thought of Jonathan Rodgers and the world tilts, her mouth ripe with vomit. She reaches into her bag, for the blue wallet, fingers rummaging to 1993, the stamp decorated with green and red pears. Clean and breezy, it cuts through the thickness. The memory is cleansed.

Coming the other way is a mother, head stiff, arm taut, yanking her daughter along. The child leans back, digging in her heels. Emma wonders what the child has done, what it was that finally made the parent's patience snap. Sharp pain shoots up Emma's arm, resting in her shoulder. She finds the spot with her fingertips and pushes down, working the muscle, loosening it bit by bit until it dulls enough to carry on.

Emma arrives at the auction house, smiles at the waitress but refuses the complimentary champagne, knowing it will taste no different than fizzy water. She opts for a seat in the centre of the back row where she can scout out the room.

She watches as new and old money collide, battling for a set of eight laminated Damien Hirst prints, a David Bowie album cover. The Penny Blacks are finally brought onstage, and the assistant snaps on a pair of blue latex gloves, holding the stamps out for the audience to see. Emma remembers the last Penny Black she tasted, a reward after securing a new client, how she had lounged back on her sofa and let her head swim in ruby-rich viscosity. Her mouth waters.

The finest example of a true British classic, says the auctioneer. We'll start the bidding at £400,000. I see £400,000. Do I have £420,000?

The speed elicits murmurs from the crowd. Emma looks from side to side, arching her neck, but cannot see the person who bid.

Any advance on £400,000?

The man in front of Emma nudges his companion, whispers something into his ear. They both turn their heads to the left and she follows the direction of their gaze towards a woman. Her hair is silver, a pixie cut with a high-quiff fringe. Pearl studs sparkle from her lobes. Red lipstick, thick black brows. Short and slight. Alone.

Going once, going twice.

Emma searches for other hands before fixing her gaze on the woman.

Sold, says the auctioneer, pounding the gavel.

It is dusk as Emma leaves the auction house, following the woman down New Bond Street, then Grosvenor Street. At Bourdon Street, the woman folds into an alleyway, leans against the wall. She is shaking as she rustles through her bag, pulling out the stamps and cupping them in her hands as if taking Communion.

She begins tentatively, tongue flicking at a corner, eyes

turning inwards, head lolling back. Her laugh is guttural, brimming with pleasure. It is when she lowers her head again, ready for more, that she sees Emma, fixing her with a knowing look.

You were at Sotheby's, she says, gliding towards Emma and lifting her chin with a fingertip tap. Deep lines surround her mouth, span her forehead. Her perfume is rich, like a 1985 Vivien Leigh. I've bought so many stamps, she says. I've been buying them all. I never knew there was another like me. She holds out her palms, pushes the stamps close. Emma stares down at the four portraits of Queen Victoria and uncoils.

There was someone, once, at the beginning of fresher's year, when Emma was buoyed by the freedom, the hope, of escaping home. He was all ribs and elbows, not handsome or sexy, but Emma would gaze out the window on the second floor of the library and watch him, day after day, enter the post office, leaving five, eight, twelve minutes later. At first, she thought it a coincidence. Then, unable to shake the thought, her mind untethered.

A month into the term, Emma's neighbour Liz turned nineteen and invited all twelve freshers from the corridor for a meal. Giddy with vodka-coke they stumbled to the bus stop, although Emma lagged behind, laden with dread. She had already looked up the menu online, settling on a Spicy Cajun pizza, praying that the peppery hit of Tabasco would shock her tastebuds to life, cut through the grease and stodge, fend off the nausea.

And there he was, at the bus stop.

Joe, he said, shaking Emma's hand. I'm on Liz's course.

The restaurant was busy, chairs crammed around the too-small table. Emma sat at the end, next to Joe, boxed in against the wall and the family behind them.

I never eat out, he whispered in her ear, his breath hot on her lobe.

Me neither, she said, before agreeing to swap numbers.

When the food arrived, Joe prodded at his lasagne, stared at the gooey fork with disgust.

Looks fucking revolting, he said.

Mine too.

Emma picked up the smallest slice, nibbled the crust, working her jaw, counting the chews until she could glug her water and wash the gloop away. But as she paused, gearing herself up for more, she realised that she didn't care whether the girls at the other end of the table were watching her; she didn't care what they were thinking.

There was a tap on her shoulder and she turned to face Joe.

To be fair, it's better than it looks, he said, mouth open, revealing thick strings of bechamel. His lasagne was half-finished.

I don't feel great, Emma replied, squeezing between the chairs and staggering outside, where the taxi driver charged her twenty pounds back to campus. Madonna woke her, at 2 a.m., blaring from the kitchen, the thumping bass, the caterwaul singalong. Emma stayed in bed.

The party lasted an hour before they killed the music, slurring goodnights and love to one another. Through paper-thin walls, Emma heard a key sticking into Liz's lock, a pile of books tumbling to the floor, the way they moaned without shame. Emma got up, took the last few booklets from her desk drawer, and ripped the stamps out six at a time. Mouth wide, she rammed them in, her head exploding in colour, as if she'd looked straight at the sun, her legs buckling beneath her. From next door, Joe gave one final grunt as Emma collapsed on top of her duvet and silence descended once more.

Go ahead, the woman says. They are delicious.

Emma places a hand on the alleyway wall, steadies herself, blood pounding in her ears, her wrists.

She licks.

A flick of a switch and everything is light, the alley bright, its fusty, fetid smell gone in an instant. Deep caramelised flavours course through her mouth. A fire ignites her belly. The woman looks on, biting her lower lip, before bowing her head and joining Emma in the tasting. Foreheads brush; breath condenses on flushing cheeks.

Sherbet sharp, their tongues touch.

You taste like a Penny Black, whispers the woman, wrapping her arms around Emma's waist as she releases her grip on the stamps.

Emma sees them fall. And, like that, she is plummeting too, towards the grot and grime, the dog-piss crevices, closer and closer until the gasp of a breeze catches her, whisks her up and over, allowing her to settle into its caress, fluttering left and right, easing her way down to the alley floor. Face up, she lands, staring skywards, head high, chin raised.

There is a moment of darkness, more than shadow, as something looms above. Pain tears through her, a blade across her jaw. A heel, a black Jimmy Choo, skittering across the cobbles as the bodies above fumble and fuss, catching her edge, ripping her mouth, pulling it higher. It is the hint of a grin but she is transformed.

The touch of skin and tongue lingers on her epidermis. And although she feels the dirt sticking to her glue, dampness seeping through, the gathering wind threatening at her edges, she has no regrets. Who wants to be shut away, temperature-controlled, feeling nothing but the stroke of a rubber glove, or the pinch of tweezers, metallic and sharp? Tonight, she will take it all in. Pleasure is not for rationing.

DAIRY FARM RAIDED BY GIANT BIRD

Sukie Wilson

Caring for my mother is difficult. The tasks themselves – feed her, wash her, tidy her space – are fairly simple. Being in the same room as her is harder. Hiding her is harder still.

I never married, never met anyone who would have me, and no one ever asked me not to live in the house my mother raised me in. I was welcome there. I left anyway. I miss my little flat above the bookie's, my hideaway. I wonder if the subletter has let my houseplants die.

She noticed almost as soon as the changes began. With her final precious days as herself, she sought to make the work ahead easier for me. She put her belongings in order, finalised her will, and wrote long goodbyes to each distant family member in progressively erratic handwriting. They all think she died months ago, now. My letter was different.

Before the change, my mother approached life as a great buffet: sample every joy, every pain, every heartbreak, and move on to the next. Let the flavours mingle on the tongue. Appreciate the unique pairing of the joy of your first and only child's birth with the achingly sudden death of your beloved husband. The phases of her life washed over her;

she let them break and retreat. I often found this deeply frustrating: she never expected me to linger on my pains, and so left me no room to do so. I remember, at thirteen, crying into her lap, distraught in that way only a teenager mid-crush can manage. She held me for ten minutes, pushed me off, and told me that eventually I would laugh about this – and she was laughing, and she expected me to laugh with her. The moment had passed and she was simply allowing the next to arrive – that's how I expect she would have explained it. I wanted her to hold me for at least another hour. I wanted her to plait my hair and tell me that I was already perfect, that I didn't need a decade's perspective and could dwell at thirteen if I wanted to. She got up and put the kettle on instead.

Now, she dwells herself in a way I know she would have hated. An awkward in-between phase with an obvious end, but no clear timetable for when that might happen. I am letting her dwell there, in the attic with no windows, in the room I claimed as my teenage bedroom. When I arrived, she had already cleared it out and locked herself in. I found the wreckage of my teens boxed and piled at the foot of the stair, and the key to my old room still in the door. I don't know how she managed to lock herself in from the inside.

In between trips upstairs with a basin and washcloth, I have been going through those boxes. Everything I had thought important enough to keep, I'd brought with me to my new home above the Ladbrokes. The boxes held the things I had wanted to leave behind: a shrine to gangly mistakes and interests I'd rather have forgotten about. With it all stuffed in the attic room, I didn't have to carry those old shames with me. I could choose to keep my GCSE certificates, and be rid of the diaries I had filled while taking the exams. I could keep the framed pressed flowers, and forget all about the girl who picked them for me. Bang bang bang through the ceiling. Off up again. I remind myself: I am doing for her what she did for her mother. I am doing what the young women of our family have done for each previous generation, maybe stretching back forever.

She left me a comprehensive guide on what to expect from her, what phases to keep an eye out for, and specific instructions on what to feed her. Once a week I take the list she wrote to the big supermarket and scour the shelves. The workers there keep moving the stock around, so I can't develop a practised route: I have to go through every aisle, see every offer on tinned goods. I dread this task, as it involves the possibility of seeing people. Not just anyone – though that would be bad enough, unshowered and in last week's stained tracky bottoms. People who used to know my mother. Or worse yet, people who used to know me.

The woman across the road, Deb, purposely times her weekly shop to coincide with mine. Her curtains flutter when I'm walking down my mother's drive. She waits until I am in a corner, distracted by the bright buzzing lights and tinny music, and pounces. She demands to know if there's anything she can do to help during my time of grief, and is the landlord letting me stay in the house much longer, and she was saddened not to be invited to the funeral but she supposed a private service must have been more appropriate, and why am I buying so much meat when we both know how the gout got my grandmother? I never see her coming, and it is all I can do to blink and flap my mouth open and closed, open and closed, hoping maybe some words might occur that way. She slaps my arm with a moist, perfumed hand, her face a picture of pitied disgust, and pretends she came to this corner for the children's cereal behind me. I flee to the next item on my mother's list: a gallon of whole milk.

Someone else is already in the milk aisle, lifting out the milk cartons at the front and leaving them in an arc on the floor around her, comparing the sell-by dates. I wonder why anyone else would need old whole milk. She sees me watching her as she leans the milk cartons atop the pile of packaged meats in her trolley.

I recognise Sandra immediately, by the shape of her eyes. Almost everything else has changed, except her bug eyes. She doesn't look well. Her short hair is stringy, and she frustratedly pushes it back from where it flops in front of her face. Her once full figure is half empty, and her athleisure is hanging off of her. I badly want to leave my trolley and run out of the supermarket, but I would have to run past her to get to the exit. She has recognised me, she has seen the contents of my trolley, and I can see by the way her jaw muscles work that she is doing a similar mental arithmetic.

'Hi' – my heart near enough falls out of my chest, she sounds just the same – 'do you want to come round for some tea?'

We don't say more until we are in her kitchen. It's not how I remember it – the wallpaper is yellowing. Maybe Sandra smokes now. She puts our bags of meats in a deep chest fridge placed awkwardly in the middle of the room, and files the milk atop the kitchen radiator. I nearly trip over the fridge power lead, but catch myself on the breakfast table. It's the same table I remember 'studying' at on school nights. She sees me looking at the Formica and I know she is remembering too, although the memory probably feels different to her. Less shame, more hurt.

'I thought you'd moved away?' she says.

'I did.'

'So did I . . .' Her mouth opens to say more, then shuts. We both look at the chest fridge.

'When did it start for yours?' She was always braver than me.

'Oh. I'm not sure, actually. I didn't find out until it had already started. Maybe four months ago?'

She nods in a pantomime of wisdom, greasy hair flapping against her forehead. 'Penny went about six months ago. I knew it would happen – I still kind of remember Gran going. Not much, y'know, I would only have been five or six, but I remember Mum drilling me on what to say at school. Mustn't say we keep Granny in the basement! No clue how she managed it, with two kids. Dad couldn't have been any help.'

I remember her father with painful clarity. Specifically, the way he would look at me over his reading glasses when we'd pass him on the way to her bedroom.

I must have made a face. She's started rummaging through dirty dishes for two mugs to rinse out.

'Can I see her?'

It was always easier to talk when she wasn't looking at me. She stops looking for mugs.

'Yeah, all right.'

*

I remembered Penny as a talkative, weirdly funny, mother. Sandra inherited her bug eyes, her thick dark hair, her curves, and her three-up-three-down-plus-basement dilapidated old terrace house. Penny had appeared to me as the kind of mother I'd been a bit green to discover actually existed. She always listened to Sandra talk about her day at school with genuine interest, and never forgot to make dinner. She was a fantastic gift-giver – she never needed a birthday list, she'd know even before you did exactly what you were missing. Her sense of humour surprised teenaged me – I didn't know mums were allowed to make jokes, never mind ones that would actually land.

When Sandra lets me into the basement, Penny is not there. In her place, in her skin, is a very large bird. *Oh, so they get birds, then.*

The floor is littered with feathers and scraps of old leathery skin. Sandra pours yellowed milk into a wide, shallow bowl in the corner of the room. The bird who had been Penny rises from her nest of blankets and pillows like a marionette, wings first. Beneath the dark feathers, her loose body gives the impression of an old duvet being shaken out. I can just see her pink nose peeking out at the top of the bird. *Still a way to go, then.* Her wings scrape the ceiling as she stretches, unsettling the musty air – there isn't enough room to unfold them completely.

'All right, Mum? You'll remember Izzy,' Sandra says, standing back from the bowl as the bird advances on it. The room lurches around me – to hear her say my name again! Bird-Penny makes no response, only drops part of her precarious body to the bowl. Sandra sighs, lightly, as if she'd already let all the air out of herself before I'd arrived.

'How much longer do you think it'll take?' I ask her.

'It's hard to say – she'd been sick before it started. Something to do with her stomach, she wouldn't tell me what, just said she hoped to go before . . . well . . .' – she gestures to the dark mass of feathers doing *something* to a bowl of off milk in the corner – 'this. It could be soon, I suppose. Hard to imagine it ever ending, now.'

There is a way about her face as she looks at her mother-bird, unfocused, almost looking through her. The single unshaded bulb lights her skin yellow, and I remember pressing buttercups under her soft, dimpled chin. It's suddenly obvious that Sandra will end up with wings.

'Do you ever think about letting her out?'

The question catches me off guard.

'What, like at night? I'd never get her back in agai–'

'No, no – I mean . . . doesn't it feel cruel to keep her like this?' She's speaking over her shoulder, halfway out the basement door. 'I know it's what she wanted, and god knows she knew what she was asking of *me* . . . It still feels like a hard thank-you for raising me.'

I slip past her into the tight square before the basement stairs, watch her deliberate over locking the door. There is no space between us. Her breath mists my glasses. I can smell her; musky, in desperate need of a shower, delicious.

I remember the last time I was this close to her face. I remember the compulsion to kiss the little space between her chin and her lips. I remember her hot hand on the back of my neck. I remember the bathroom door swinging open. I remember the laughter, the shame – my god, the burning shame. I remember the clamouring to distance myself, pushing her away, pushing her over, pushing her into blame, pushing her into years of isolation and bullying. I remember the shame, like touching a hot coal in the furnace of my mind.

'I'm so sorry,' I whisper. It feels like a secret, to be spoken softly.

'It'll come to us all.' She shrugs.

'No, I mean – when we were kids. I should have kissed you again.'

'Oh,' and her expression is so genuine, a flower blooming over her features, I have to kiss her. More than that – I want to. Her lips are peeling – beautiful. I take the key from her rough hand, slip it tenderly into the breast pocket of her Lycra top, just over her heart. I want to hold her, and to see what sounds she might make if I curl my fingers just right. I want everyone to hear us. She opens her mouth and gasps into mine. I swallow the sound.

The clock in the hall strikes. The rest of the world rushes in past it – four o'clock, my own mother will be screeching for her own bowl of sour, lumpy milk soon. The idea that anyone might hear us curdles, sends lightning down my spine. For a moment as I withdraw, Sandra looks as though she has fallen asleep standing up. Closed eyes, dry mouth ajar, muscles slackened. A sweet dream, which vanishes as she wakes to see the truth of me in this dim stairwell. Her jaw closes, her brow furrows. I cannot bear her judgement again.

I have the presence of mind to take my shopping from the fridge before I run. I clasp the flimsy plastic bags of meat and milk to my chest and sprint through the same alleys I'd always taken as a teen, where the houses seem to lean politely away. Like I had been staring at a light bulb,

I cannot wipe Sandra's face from the back of my eyes: resigned, and not surprised. I am nearing a junction, just two turns till my street, when of course, one of the bags rips loudly. I scrabble to grab the packaged meat, succeed in time to realise I have not caught the milk, and feel it splash up my legs to soak my tracksuit and trainers. I hear a high laugh, and swivel my head to the sound – in a window at the back of a house, overlooking the junction, net curtains swish back into place. Deb's house. I leave the milk where it pooled on the pavement.

I finally reach the front garden, and I cringe so hard my face might turn inside out. I can hear my mother groaning from here. There are eyes boring into the back of my head. I hunch my shoulders to them and shuffle in as fast as the precarious bags permit. Inside the sound is worse. The neighbours either side must have been able to hear every quaking syllable. She must be so thirsty. Her letter had been pointedly specific: only milk. I grab the last soured carton, half emptied, from the radiator by the stairs. My feet lead me up to the attic door.

It has been months. It could be a year before the transformation ends. I hold the key in my hand and think of Sandra's Lycra pocket, atop her sweet heart. How wonderful it would be, to have everyone know how I think of her. How terrible. How terrifyingly wonderful. I put the key in the lock.

Fool's Gold

Sean Bell

'For now I ask no more than the justice of eating.'
– Pablo Neruda

It was Christmas Eve. The glow of the restaurant cut through the blizzard like the moon through a midnight sea.

Wayne parked the shuddering burnt-orange Cadillac as carefully as he was able and got out. Tornadic snow whipping at the grey woollen overcoat he'd picked up from a Salvation Army three states past – sleeves long enough to cover most of his hands, the rest long enough to cover a sawn-off shotgun when necessary – he opened the passenger door for Odessa, his sweetheart. A cowboy boot extended, as if anticipating a red carpet.

It would not be difficult to peg the lovers as unprepared for their first Colorado winter. If Wayne's threadbare coat and unfastened trapper hat were insufficient for the elements, the tiger-print, faux-fur jacket that barely reached Odessa's wasp-like waist was an insult to the gods of weather.

He wrapped one arm around her shivering shoulder and guided her through the storm, towards the dream she'd held since she was twelve years old.

The state of Mississippi has the highest rate of food poverty in the country. One in four children across the state go hungry. Recent studies estimate those facing such deprivation collectively require an additional $273,100,000 per year to meet their basic needs.

Following their withdrawal the previous morning, Odessa and Wayne were now $197,350 closer to meeting that goal.

The restaurant was one of Denver's oldest and most popular eateries, but the blizzard had seen a few of its festive reservations cancelled, so the hostess who greeted the young couple was able to find them a cosy red-leather booth near the kitchen, its table lamp spilling an oasis of liquid gold across the rosewood. Promptly, a waitress brought them their menus, a complimentary breadbasket, and a Dr Pepper for Wayne.

'D'you think we should get a cat?' Odessa asked.

Her boyfriend looked thoughtful for a moment, then replied: 'Not sure if it's really a matter of "should". Do you *want* a cat?'

'I do. And I think New Orleans is a "cat" kind of town. Would you mind livin' with a cat?'

'Half the time, I already do,' Wayne said, returning to his study of the laminated menu.

Odessa picked up a bread roll and motioned to throw it at him, but did not.

Odessa's upbringing would have been Southern Gothic, but

they could never afford it.

Her mother's appetites denied Odessa's own; Odessa never forgave her for that. She also never forgave her for the stories her mother would tell, whenever she reached her own personal twilight, and the pills inspired great poetry and visions in the prone woman on the past-stained, fold-out sofa bed. When, for days at a time, those multicoloured little capsules were all that would pass her lips – lips that would explicate the grand conspiracies of life, against which no honest person had a chance – she would talk of her diner days.

She would tell of cheeseburgers and fries, chicken and waffles, steak and eggs, biscuits and gravy, smothered pork chops and country fried ham, stacks of pancakes and racks of ribs. She would tell of legendary secret recipes (which she would never share) and techniques passed down from grandmothers (though never her own).

And then, inevitably, she would be diverted into recounting how Roosevelt (the sinister short-order cook with the janky prison ink) and Alicia (that bitch head waitress who thought she was better than she was) had used the vital necessity of her pain management regimen against her, and plotted the injustice of her ejection into a purgatory of welfare and woe.

By that point, however, her daughter would have stopped listening. As she finished heating up whatever she had managed to shoplift, Odessa would instead be thinking about how the only time she ever tasted Manwich mix with actual meat in it was in the school cafeteria – that is, before they cut her off as a debtor's child.

*

The restaurant served the sort of cuisine that might be expected by middle-class Denverites prepared to splash out on something lavish yet familiar – shrimp cocktail, filet mignon, Colorado-style venison chilli – but amongst this selection, unchanged since the days when Richard Nixon roamed the Earth, it did offer one novelty, which endured more out of historical significance than actual demand.

Odessa did not need to examine the menu. She knew exactly what to order.

A long time ago, Elvis Presley lived in a magical place called Graceland, where one night he was entertaining two friends from Colorado who told him about a sandwich called the Fool's Gold.

Invented in a Denver restaurant that had decided to introduce some whimsicality to its bill of fare, the Fool's Gold is an entire loaf of Italian white bread, hollowed out, then filled with a whole jar of peanut butter, a whole jar of grape jelly, and a solid pound of crispy bacon. Traditionally, the sandwich is accompanied by a bottle of vintage champagne.

So bewitched was Elvis by the idea of the Fool's Gold, he and his friends departed immediately for the King's private jet and flew directly to Denver. When they arrived at 1:40 a.m., they were greeted by the restaurant's owners, who carried with them twenty-two freshly made Fool's Gold sandwiches. The feast lasted for three hours.

Odessa grew up in Tupelo, Mississippi, where Elvis was born and from which he escaped. That was one of the reasons she loved him. The story of the Fool's Gold was another.

Odessa wasn't the only one who thought that Wayne, with his black sideburns and soulful eyes, looked like a skinny Elvis. Tonight, however, she wanted to eat like a fat one.

'The Fool's Gold, please,' Odessa told the waitress. 'With the Dom *Pérignon*.'

She placed emphasis on the last word, resolute in her determination not to mispronounce it, thus achieving a cadence not dissimilar to a Cajun poet speaking to a long-distance operator. With nary a raised eyebrow, the waitress nodded silently, then left the young lovers to themselves. Wayne smiled at Odessa, and she smiled at him.

'Do you think they have hockey in New Orleans?' he asked.

Odessa cocked her head. 'I didn't think you liked hockey.'

'Yeah, but who knows? I might take an interest. New things and all.'

'Yeah.' As a silver ice bucket was set down beside their table, Odessa shrugged. 'New things and all.'

Bank robberies were supposed to be difficult, and perhaps they were. The trick, as far as Odessa could tell, was to be determined, undistracted and above all, quick about your work.

Wayne was all of those things, and always had been. In the past, this had helped keep him in more regular employment than some others with whom they grew up, who didn't live lives as such, but instead played unwilling roles in a satire on capitalism at which no one – no one they knew, anyway – was laughing.

Nevertheless, those qualities everyone so admired in Wayne – the ones, they always commented, which stood in such sharp contrast with those of his late, misbegotten father – only ever took him so far . . . at least, on the side of the law he had left behind without regret the previous morning.

Wayne's family technically wasn't as poor as Odessa's, in the sense they technically had more money to lose, if only for a brief moment each week. During that recurrent moment – with Wayne left in whatever motel they were staying at while his mother was back in Tupelo, punishing a dentist's office typewriter – his father would go down to the nearest dog track, walk into the betting office, and almost invariably walk out with less money than when he went in.

The day before, Wayne had walked into a bank, and walked out with almost two hundred grand more than when he went in. Wayne considered this a generational improvement.

The Fool's Gold was the size of a World War II tank shell. The waitress placed it between them with a mischievous touch of ceremony before sliding a bread knife down the middle like it was a birthday cake. Wayne covered his glass when she made to pour the champagne.

'I'm drivin',' he said, then glanced at the blizzard beyond the window. 'In theory, anyhow.'

For an infinite moment, Odessa just looked at the vast, gooey slab on her plate. People who sneer and joke about sweating in Vegas and dying on the toilet, she reflected, never really understood. There are those in this world who do not see the King's final years as a sad decline, but as the gold at the end of a rainbow so many others can only stare up at. Maybe they're fools, but there are worse things to be.

When you reach the end of that rainbow, you do everything you ever wanted to do, where once before you could not.

For some people – a lot of people, where Odessa and Wayne were raised – that meant eating like you didn't care. Specifically, like you didn't care how much was left for tomorrow; about whether more calories per mouthful could've been purchased for the same couple of dollars; about how many cans of Dinty Moore beef stew and SpaghettiOs you could cram into your pockets before the store clerk noticed.

In her dreams, these concerns would be replaced by new ones, and she could care about other things. Things like how *good* food can taste, or how it can feel to be so full and sated you could sleep for a hundred years, or how no one – *no one* – should ever reach the end of a so-called meal and still feel hungry, or consider the act of eating a mere exercise in tenuous survival.

As even Elvis knew, the Fool's Gold is not a meal for a single person – this, Odessa understood. She would no more consume it alone than she would have robbed a bank without her boyfriend by her side. There are some things you can only do with other people.

'Let's eat,' she said.

Odessa had heard it argued – by whom, she couldn't remember – that good food tastes of everything in its past: of traditions and culture, labour and invention; of things that grew in the soil, hung upon the vine and sat beneath the sun. Yet when Odessa bit into that mass of potential arterial blockage, she didn't taste any of that.

She especially didn't taste those things she'd decided she never would again – radioactive-orange box mac 'n' cheese, sad and sloppy cinnamon-sugar toast, bologna that looked like long pig, tater tots frozen into fossilisation and canned Vienna sausage the consistency of plasticine. Instead, she tasted the future.

She tasted a thousand more restaurants, and the ten thousand meals they would eat in them. Po' boys made in front of her, from which amber-battered crawfish bloomed like forest fungi, so fresh from the fryer they glimmered with diamond dewdrops of fat; pillowy beignets as soft as a summer cloud and dusted like a cocaine mirror; gumbo brewed in magic cauldrons which held all that crawled upon the earth and swam in the sea, layered with an encyclopaedia of spice and seasoning that would enlighten the tongue and warm the soul; real French wine she would share with real French friends, whom she could understand and who could understand her in turn; Sazerac rye in a crystal glass with a bottom as thick and heavy as the one her gluttony would cultivate upon the frame whose bones she'd never let show again.

Odessa's reverie was first broken by her boyfriend's voice, and then by the glare of red and blue light through the restaurant windows.

'Damn,' said Wayne, masticating like a hamster in slow motion. 'That's a hell of a sandwich.'

It was, Odessa decided, a pretty good hostage situation. She was glad there were no crying children, because that was the kind of thing she would have had a hard time ignoring while she ate.

Given the circumstances, the clientele of the restaurant were acquitting themselves well. She felt a little bad for the girl who served them, though – Odessa knew being a waitress was a hard job at the best of times, so she resolved not to bother her for the rest of the evening, unless it was to pass her compliments to the chef.

'You should've brought the shotgun,' Odessa mumbled, mouth still full, as Wayne adjusted the dinky snub-nosed revolver over which he was convinced the pawnshop had ripped him off.

'Couldn't exactly hide it down my pants, could I?'

'Why not? They'd just assume what I usually do.' She grinned, wiping a beauty spot of jelly from her cheek before licking it from her finger. 'And I'm usually right.'

At this, Wayne gave a complicated sigh, and turned back to his hostages.

'We're all just going to sit tight, y'hear?' he said. 'Until the lady has finished her dinner.'

When her plate was finally clean, Odessa poured out what was left of the bottle and drained her glass. She was pleased to discover that she liked champagne, which meant – logically speaking – she was the *kind of woman* who liked champagne. Maybe money did buy class. Then again, maybe she'd had it all along.

She dabbed the sides of her mouth with her red-and-white paper napkin, stifled a silent belch, and rose from the table, beatifically bloated and glowing like a cosmic saint.

Their waitress recoiled slightly when she approached, so Odessa tried to put her at ease.

'Look at it like this, sugah,' Odessa said. 'Give it a month or so, and people will be right curious about a restaurant good enough that two bank robbers on the run stopped by for dinner.'

From within her coat, Odessa produced a stack of bills – still bearing an American Bankers Association strap – peeled off one thousand dollars in C-notes, and pressed them into the waitress's trembling hand.

'That's a tip. Don't you mention it to no one,' she whispered. 'Merry Christmas.'

As they left the restaurant and returned to the cold of the world, hands raised above their heads, Odessa knew that they weren't going to make it to New Orleans; that their days would not be an endless dance from bed to dinner and back; that they would not spend next Christmas dropping off parcels of food at the local church for those who had none, before driving off in their Cadillac to a *Réveillon* supper. Odessa knew all that, and perhaps she always had – because that's what happens when you go looking for Fool's Gold.

As they slipped the handcuffs on, she looked back at the restaurant, and spoke softly through the falling snow.

'Thank you,' she said. 'Thank you very much.'

Aqua Vitae

Karrish Devan

Irish moss, bladder wrack, furbellow. She whispered their names. *Gutweed, sugar kelp, dulse.* Incantations to resurrect the dead. *Dabberlocks, sloke, wakame.* Below Sara, the sand was stained with drops of blood. Reaching into a rock pool to fish out a piece of sea glass, something unseen had cut her. She held the glass tight in the throne of her hand. Deliciously smooth, it would fetch a good price.

In the dusk, the ladder to the pier greeted her with a glimmer. On the last rung she lost her grip, the grains of rust grating across her arm. Her mouth filled with salt. By the time she found her breath again, the water was already touching the top of her boots.

The high street was deserted when she arrived in town, the shutters humming in the wind. Sara looked up at one of the storefronts, still august with a single curved window and delicate wooden engravings. It took a while for her to remember that it had once been a stationery shop. Her son, who loved origami, would go each year and pick out sheets of Japanese paper for his birthday. Next door was the laundrette, which closed suddenly last year. Inside there were piles of neatly folded clothes, alongside the slumbering machines and potted plants crisping behind the glass.

Only the bank was open. Harsh electric light spilled out from it, across its marble steps. Once they were sharp, but many hurried feet had chewed the stone to softness. A queue snaked out of the entrance. Mostly women, old like Sara, heads cowed. Sara joined them, inching forward. The line tensed as someone at the front started crying. With hot tears of rage, she slammed her fists down on the table. Her card had expired. Sara closed her eyes; every day it grew harder to watch. It didn't take much now for her own fear to rise up. Huge and consuming, like a leviathan. Dragging her down to the depths. Screams brought her back to the room. The woman was being pulled away by the guards, likely never to be seen again. Perhaps this was a better fate, though, than the streets.

The parcel was smaller than last week's. Its contents rolled out onto Sara's kitchen counter. A dented can of beans, two packets of oats and nine ounces of jerky. She opened her larder, sighing at its barren offering. Pushing past a few empty jars, she extracted a packet of laver, the last of her dried seaweed. The sea was no longer providing, and she was no longer nimble enough to climb over the broken groynes on the beach. Gathering her coat, she went out again, to see if Marco would trade anything for the jerky. Or just repair any of her torn clothing.

She knocked next door and waited for a response, pulling

her coat tighter against the sharp fingers of the wind. The door was unlocked but her greeting rang hollow. She knew what the emptiness meant. On the kitchen table was a cardboard box with her name on it. She carried it out onto the balcony, past the collapsed armchair where a crossword rested, forever unfinished.

Leaning against the wall that separated Marco's flat from her own, she opened the box. Inside were pairs of darned socks, a waterproof tarp and, buried deeply, a tub of powdered chocolate. She held it close to her chest, like a blessing. He had gone on his own terms, like they had always joked. She left the flat, reminding herself that she could not go down to the pier for a few days now.

There was a child outside her own door when she returned. He was Safiye's, a woman Sara had a growing friendship with. Safiye and the boy herded goats, exchanging their homemade cheeses for Sara's sea salt. The boy's face was stern but his quivering eyes betrayed him. A resolve was as thin as aluminium. She offered her hand but he sprinted away, motioning for her to follow. *Samphire, sea kale, gorse.* She muttered under her breath. The names did not help dissipate her unease. *Purslane, buckthorn, alexanders.* She had not seen Safiye for a few weeks. Sara was not ready to think about another corpse.

He led her to their house on the old golf course, unlocking the door with a key tied around his neck. Before they could enter, a goat shot out. It settled outside, chewing on a piece of carpet tile. Upstairs, Sara heard coughing and caught the stench of wet hay.

'You are not a doctor,' Safiye called down, an unseen

voice from the bedroom.

'Now you sound like my father.'

Safiye laughed in response, before coughing again.

'Can you take him?' she said.

'I have little left.'

'He can milk the herd tomorrow.'

'We'll come back in the morning,' Sara said.

'No.'

'He'll want to see you again,' Sara said.

'Not like this.'

The boy would not settle in Sara's flat. He rested for mere seconds before fluttering between the rooms, disturbing stacks of books and unironed laundry. Sara poured him some water from the filter, but he just gazed back at her, eyes unwavering like an idol. In the kitchen, his stares became so intense that Sara found herself talking mindlessly.

'Now I'm just soaking the laver,' she said. 'It's a type of seaweed which we'll use to make bread.'

He looked on as Sara measured out the oats and hot water, before mixing in the laver. She pulled out a handful of the dough and shaped it into a patty, which was then left to rest near the stove. In response, the boy opened his hands expectantly. She placed a small sphere of the mixture in his palm. He dropped it instantly.

'That's hot,' he said, with a strong Scouse accent.

'Teflon hands,' Sara said, while dabbing his palm with the corner of her jumper, in a hope to assuage his tears.

'It doesn't even look like bread.'

'You're right. What would you call it?'

'Cake,' he said, smiling. 'Soggy cake.'

He was more talkative whilst Sara fried the dough. As she got out two plates, he jumped to the table and started laying out cutlery and glasses. She cut one of the cooling buns in half before passing it to him. There was a cautious nibble before he pushed the entire piece into his mouth.

'Salty,' he said.

'That's the seaweed.'

'Will Mam die?'

Sara tried to avoid his limitless eyes, instead playing with her piece of laverbread. It really wasn't that salty. The boy would have to get used to it.

'She says you're Indian,' he said.

'English for longer.'

'But your name is Sara?'

'They found it easier to say, so it stuck.'

'People call me Aaron here, but it's not my name. Why do you make seaweed?'

'I'm more of a farmer.'

'At school they said India was once a hot place. Before the water.'

'The sea is for everyone,' she said, but he looked confused. 'Like your cheese.'

'Mam says that our cheese is Turkish.'

'Where are your goats from?'

'I don't know.'

'Well, if the milk is from England and your mother is from Turkey, what does that make the cheese?'

'Halloumi,' he said, completely stone-faced.

Quite unexpectedly, Sara found herself filled with warmth for the child. It burnt brightly before sitting uncomfortably in her chest.

'She'll get better, don't worry, Aaron.'

'It's Haroon.'

'Mine is Saraswathi.'

He excused himself from the table before falling asleep on the sofa. Sara watched him snoring for a moment, before throwing a blanket over his little body.

Sleep, though, was more difficult for her to find. She dug out a bundle of postcards from under her bed. Innocuous at first glance, they appeared to have been sent from women who had remained in other seaside towns. But Sara recognised a familiar sharpness in the handwriting. Taking her time, she scored the corner of each, before peeling back a layer of the postcard. The first few had nothing inside. Then in one, there was a tightly folded letter. It was from her son. She held it to her face, hoping for some of his scent. Or at least him as a child. Antiseptic cream on grazed knees. Sticky ice cream kisses. The sweetness of his tight embraces. But the letter had no smell. Rather it detailed his escape to one of the Centres. The rest of his words flew past her, weeks of his life condensed into sentences. Hiding from the conscripts, paying a trafficker with her wedding jewellery, finding a semblance of safety in the Highlands. He begged her to join him, to find a way back together.

She could not, though. Sara told herself it was because she belonged here. In this town and this flat where she had raised him alone. Finding too her own sense of freedom. If everyone just left, then what would become of a place? Buildings were unable to hold our memories.

The truth was hidden in the tempest of her mind. Unspeakable and buried. Perhaps none of us deserved to escape. We all needed punishment after our years of indifference, allowing bodies to fall into the ocean like raindrops. Innocent people, they were easy to mistake for tributes. Sacrifices to appease an unknowable God. Now the waters surged across the world, blood red and hungry. Clawing up onto land and drowning cities. Sara pushed the letter under her pillow and closed her eyes. Then she tried, unsuccessfully, to not dream of him.

When Sara awoke, Haroon was in the kitchen, sitting by a steaming bucket of goat's milk. He remained silent throughout breakfast, despite her making a luxurious porridge. Even when she suggested that they go to find the doctor before seeing his mother, he only nodded in agreement.

Unusually, the doors to the surgery were padlocked shut when they arrived. Sara ground a piece of rubble with her boot. Despite this doctor sticking around the longest, Sara still found it difficult to trust her. She knew they just rotated between the Centres and outside. They used to call it outreach; now it was just charity. They waited for a few minutes before Sara caught the rare smell of cigarettes. She found the doctor at the back of the building, sitting on the roof of a corroded sports car. The doctor offered a brief smile, before jumping down in a defeated way. Haroon ran over, touching the doctor's elbow in familiarity. In return, she lifted him upside down, exposing the hollow of his belly. Sara noticed the doctor's travel rucksack and the strange look in her eye.

'You lasted longer than the others,' Sara said.

'I grew up here. Everyday we'd go to the beach. The sea was different then. Friendly.'

'It was always dangerous.'

'Not like this. We've all sat on this for so long. Like boiling frogs.'

'Some of us have been trying to survive.'

'Safiye likely has brucellosis,' the doctor said. 'It's an infection, from the goats.'

In front of them, Haroon was clambering up the car. Although it appeared that he was absorbed in his own world, Sara knew how much children heard. The doctor passed over a bundle of medication, tied with a piece of string.

'How often does she need to take these?'

'The antibiotics she needs don't exist anymore,' the doctor said. 'These are all I have.'

Sara looked at the tablets. Paracetamol and aspirin, both at least three years out of date.

'I hear the Centres aren't near the water,' she said, giving the doctor the sea glass she found yesterday. It glinted in the sunlight, like gold.

'Look after them,' the doctor said, before hugging Sara unexpectedly. Underneath her jumper she was nothing more than cotton and bones.

Back home, Sara sat Haroon down at the table with a set of crayons and old sheets of newspaper. He drew happily, mostly scenes of goats. *Rosehip, elderflower, honeysuckle.* Sara put the milk to boil. *Wild garlic, bramble, sweet chestnut.* What would she tell the child? *Chickweed, dandelion, witch hazel.*

'Are you praying?' he said.

'In a way.'

'What do the words mean?'

'There used to be lots of plants you could use or eat around here. Sometimes I say their names, so we don't forget.'

He did not respond and continued to draw. Sara opened the tub of chocolate powder, finding enough for just the two of them. She spooned it into the pan, the powder scattering across the surface. Gently whisked, everything soon came together.

'What's that?' said Haroon.

Sara turned, seeing that he was pointing out of the window at a dark speck in the distance.

'Blackpool Tower. It used to be full of lights.'

She placed a cup of hot chocolate next to him on the table. Over his drawings he had written his mother's name repeatedly. Tessellating like a mosaic. She turned away from him, her tears falling onto her hands. Outside, the sea was receding with the rising sun. Soon they would go to the beach and Sara would start to teach him everything she knew. Then they would come home, to eat.

Contributors' Bios

Sean Bell is a writer and poet based in Edinburgh, a graduate of the University of Stirling and of Edinburgh Napier's Creative Writing MA. His journalism has appeared in numerous publications that no longer exist, though a causal link has yet to be established.

Danny Beusch is a short-story writer who lives in Birmingham, UK. He was a finalist for the 2021 Manchester Fiction Prize, and has also been shortlisted for the Cambridge Short Story Prize, the Leicester Writes Short Story Prize, the Bridport Prize, and the Bath Flash Fiction Award. Links to his work can be found at www.dannybeusch.co.uk.

Rosie Chen is based in London and represented by Kat Aitken at Lexington Literary. Her stories have been shortlisted for the Desperate Literature Short Fiction Prize and the *Guardian* and 4th Estate 4thWrite Prize. She is working on her first novel, which was a finalist in Hachette UK's Mo Siewcharran Prize.

Jane 'Connie' Coneybeer is a California-born and

Edinburgh-based writer. One of seven children, she explores themes of family and belonging in her writing (and finds it impossible not to include an animal – or ten – in every story). She was shortlisted for the 2023 Cymera Prize for Speculative Short Fiction and has been published in *From Arthur's Seat* Volume VIII.

Louie Conway is a writer living in South-East London. He earned a master's degree in creative writing from Birkbeck, University of London, in 2023, and is currently working on a novel.

Karrish Devan is a writer and junior doctor based in East London. His work explores hidden histories and stories of migration, through the lens of literary fiction. This year his novel-in-progress was shortlisted for Stormzy's #Merky Books New Writers' Prize and awarded New Writing North's A Writing Chance prize.

Kate Ellis is a writer based in London. She has an MA in creative writing from Birkbeck and her short fiction has been published in the *Open Pen Anthology*, *The Mechanics' Institute Review* and *The London Short Story Prize Anthology* among others. She runs the Brick Lane Bookshop Short Story Prize, works for Inpress Books, and one day might finish writing her short-story collection.

Karishma Jobanputra is a British Indian writer based in London. A graduate of Columbia University's MFA Fiction programme, she has been listed for the Disquiet Literary Prize for Fiction twice and was awarded the 2021 Eilean

Shona Writing Workshop Scholarship, returning there to teach in 2023. Her work has been published in *No Tokens Journal*, *wildness* and *Pigeon Pages*, among other places. She is currently working on a collection of short stories and a novel.

Denise Jones, HonDLitt, FRSA, Freeman of the City of London, studied graphic design, was a primary school teacher and has worked with the bookshop that she co-founded since 1978. She lives in Cable Street and was an elected Labour councillor in Tower Hamlets from 1994 to 2022. Denise strongly supports the arts and is a board member of Rich Mix, Trinity Buoy Wharf Trust and Mulberry Schools Trust. She is Deputy Chair of the Portal Trust, where she chairs the Grants committee, and Chair of the Aldgate & Allhallows Foundation. She has served on the boards of the Arts Council, Museum of London, Whitechapel Art Gallery, Create London, Lee Valley Regional Park Authority, Young V&A and other trusts.

Sharmaine Lim is a writer from London. She is a member of the London Library's Emerging Writers Programme 2024/25, and recently completed an MA in creative writing at UEA. Her short fiction has been shortlisted for the Bridport and Fish prizes. She is working on a novel and a short-story cycle, exploring themes such as gender roles under patriarchy, complex family relationships and cross-cultural lives. She was formerly a tax lawyer.

David McGrath is from Wicklow in Ireland. His story 'The Birth of a Devil Sheep' is set in the fictitious town of Ballybalt in surroundings much like Wicklow. The story is a prologue plucked from his novel *The Crack*, which is almost finished. He lives in London.

Ali Roberts is a Devon-born fiction writer. His work has been published with *STORGY Magazine* and *The Mechanics' Institute Review*, shortlisted for the 2022 Bridport Prize, the last ever (2019) *Glimmer Train* Short Story Award for New Writers, and longlisted for the 2021 *Short Fiction Journal* Prize.

Born and raised in Aotearoa New Zealand, **Laura Surynt** is a teacher and writer. She is currently working on a novel.

Sukie Wilson is a London-based writer, working around the slowed time of chronic illness. Their work has been shortlisted for Spread the Word's Early Career Bursary and the Alpine Fellowship Writing Prize. Sukie is the winner of the 2024 Desperate Literature Prize for Short Fiction. They are a multi-tasker by nature, so Sukie is currently working on both a collection of short stories and their first novel.

Judges' Bios

Dan Bird joined Granta in July 2019. After initially working as part of Granta's campaigns team, he moved into the editorial department in 2021. As an editor, he acquires across both fiction and non-fiction. Recent titles on which he's worked include Holly Pester's *The Lodgers*, Sam Mills' *The Watermark*, Justin Torres' *Blackouts*, and Walter Kempowski's *An Ordinary Youth* (translated by Michael Lipkin), as well as forthcoming work from Anastasiia Fedorova, Mónica Ojeda, Luis López Carrasco and Lim Solah. Prior to joining Granta, he worked at Waterstones, as both a bookseller and events coordinator, while completing an MA in contemporary literature at Queen Mary University of London.

Lucy Luck is an agent of literary fiction and non-fiction at C&W. She joined in 2016 having previously worked at Aitken Alexander Associates, Lucy Luck Associates (which she founded in 2006) and Rogers, Coleridge & White. Her list of authors includes Douglas Stuart, Catherine O'Flynn, Rowan Hisayo Buchanan, Colin Barrett, Kevin Barry, Sara Baume, Richard Beard, Colin Walsh, Sara Taylor, Roddy Doyle, Wendy Erskine, Zoe Gilbert, Eley Williams, Garth

Greenwell and Andrew Michael Hurley.

Vanessa Onwuemezi is a writer living in London. She is the winner of *The White Review* Short Story Prize 2019 and her work has appeared in literary and art magazines, including *Granta*, *Frieze* and *Prototype*. Her debut story collection, *Dark Neighbourhood*, published in 2021, was named one of the *Guardian*'s Best Books of 2021 and was shortlisted for both the Republic of Consciousness Prize and the Edge Hill Prize in 2022. Her short story 'Green Afternoon' was shortlisted for the BBC National Short Story Award 2022.

Judges' Quotes

On the Anthology

'These stories are alive, conjuring distinct and refreshing worlds. They're unexpected and inventive, and wonderfully demonstrate just how capacious the short-story form can be.'

Dan Bird

'It was a pleasure to be introduced to these twelve new voices. Each story surprised, entertained and moved me in unpredictable ways and each writer brought a finesse and a sense of adventure to the story form which was fascinating to experience. I am confident all who read this anthology will find many things to admire here, and some things to love.'

Lucy Luck

'At times challenging, comical, and raw, the stories in this anthology are an excellent showcase of the short form.'

Vanessa Onwuemezi

1st Prize

Menagerie – Jane Coneybeer

'The writing is breathless, tense, and lived, with a nice physicality to it.'

Dan Bird

'The form works perfectly for this story and the moment of realisation is brilliantly effective.'

Lucy Luck

'Excellent, moving, original storytelling. A skilful use of the form melding animal folklore and mysticism.'

Vanessa Onwuemezi

2nd Prize

Un – Louie Conway

'Nice clinical eye and very impressive control – these movements between the microbial and the existential; the looping between fundamentals and chance. Excellent voice.'

Dan Bird

'Beautifully written and powerful. Assured and strong.'

Lucy Luck

'A great demonstration of the short form's flexibility with skilful dilation of time. It reminded me of Tobias Wolff's

'Bullet in the Brain'. Technically brilliant.'

                                                 Vanessa Onwuemezi

3rd Prize

The Birth of a Devil Sheep – David McGrath

'Enjoyed this a lot. Frenetic, lewd, ludic, rude, a little silly. The cyclical structure really works, and effectively taps into storytelling traditions / oral history / gossip.'

                                                          Dan Bird

'A story of antic energies and excellent dialogue in the tradition of the best of contemporary Irish short-story writers.'

                                                  Lucy Luck

'Reminds me of what I love about short stories, playful, comical, strange and with a great ending.'

                                             Vanessa Onwuemezi

Shortlisted Stories

A Love Story – Karishma Jobanputra

'Breathless, heady voice. It reminded me of Hanya Yanagihara's lifestyle focus in places. The story is baked into the city and baked into what they're consuming. Compelling reading.'

                                                          Dan Bird

Green – Laura Surynt

'A story that is beautifully written.'

Lucy Luck

The Second Can Wait – Sharmaine Lim

'The opening is wonderfully insular, claustrophobic, and there's a striking physicality to the text. Something of a Ferrante about it. The mundanity and matter-of-factness of the sterilisation narrative is chilling.'

Dan Bird

Longlisted Stories

Aqua Vitae – Karrish Devan

'Engaging, and the writing captured my interest all the way through. The dystopian themes were introduced subtly, with strong world building.'

Vanessa Onwuemezi

DAIRY FARM RAIDED BY GIANT BIRD – Sukie Wilson

'A good, original concept and well written.'

Vanessa Onwuemezi

Fool's Gold – Sean Bell

'Impressive dialogue and a story that lands.'

Lucy Luck

Glue – Danny Beusch

'Love the pitch and core idea of this one – it's lively, fresh and fun, and the ending scene is wonderfully done.'

Dan Bird

Heroes of the South West – Ali Roberts

'Skilful use of the form incorporating parallel stories and a nice exposition of the writing process which works really well.'

Vanessa Onwuemezi

Keiko and I – Rosie Chen

'Really nice voice and good character work. It's sharp, pellucid; simple, but effective.'

Dan Bird

Writers' Endorsements

'Being awarded the third-place prize in the BLB Short Story Prize 2022 had a real impact on my writing life. It was not only a vote of confidence in my writing from a team of judges that I respected and admired, but it also led to me meeting my literary agent, which was a huge step forward in my writing career.'

Emily Gaywood-James, 2022 3rd Prize

'Writing is often an isolating vocation and winning the Brick Lane Bookshop Short Story Prize gave me validation for my work and allowed me to connect with other writers. I'd recommend it to anyone!'

Imogen Fox, 2022 1st Prize

'An amazing, affirming experience. It was a completely joyous surprise to have my work read and held carefully by the competition team and the judges. It's such a beautiful feeling to know that people have read your work and somehow connected with it, seen something in it and want to celebrate it.'

Isha Karki, 2019 shortlist

'Writing can feel quite lonesome, strange, insane – so for me, this competition meant: there's something worthwhile about it. Keep at it, said the announcement. Keep at it, said the book on my shelf. And keep at it, said every response from everyone who read my words. Thanks to the Brick Lane Bookshop Short Story Prize, I keep on keeping at it.'

Kieran Toms, 2020 2nd Prize

'Winning third place in the Brick Lane Bookshop Short Story Prize was a vital confidence boost at the start of my writing career. I consider it a turning point – the moment I went from writing as a hobby to believing I could do this as a journey.'

Harper Walton, 2023 3rd Prize

'Winning the BLB Short Story Prize 2023 was a complete surprise, and all the sweeter for it. This is one of my very favourite prizes – it's clear that everyone involved, from first readers to judges, really values and understands short stories and those who write them, generously rewarding long- and shortlistees with paid publication and support for their writing. I also appreciate the rare feature of a 5,000 word limit, offering writers space to go short or longer. The only thing to do is write your story and enter!'

K. Lockwood Jefford, 2023 winner, 2020 3rd Prize

'I'll never forget the launch party: my story, with my name, in so many books in so many hands. All because I walked past a poster in the window of Brick Lane Bookshop and thought, "What's the worst that could happen?"'

James Mitchell, 2019 winner

'I think, quite simply, that the BLB Prize made me feel I might not be entirely insane to try and do this writing thing.'

JP Pangilinan-O'Brien, 2021 shortlist

'The Brick Lane Bookshop Prize is a truly great prize. The anthologies are of such a high standard, always a pleasure to read and to hold.'

Leeor Ohayon, 2023 2nd Prize, 2021 shortlist

'Entering the Brick Lane Bookshop Short Story Prize was the best thing I did in 2021. I spent so long convincing myself that I wasn't a "real writer" and it is hard to express in words how much being shortlisted in 2021 buoyed my confidence. Seeing my name in print was exhilarating and I got to meet some other lovely and talented writers in the process. I cannot recommend it enough. If you are even slightly considering it, apply! Only good things can come of it.'

Nayela Wickramasuriya, 2021 shortlist

'Being shortlisted gave me confidence in myself and it also led to much bigger things that were out of my control. It was really important.'

Huma Qureshi, 2020 shortlist

'Winning the competition was such a confidence boost. Validation from other writers, editors and agents pushes you to consider your work as valuable and worth the time that you're putting into it. It was such a joy and an honour and I was so grateful to have won it.'

Aoife Inman, 2021 winner

Thanks

Every writer who submitted a story to the competition.

The forty long-longlisted writers who made our job so enjoyable and difficult.

The twelve longlisted writers whose excellent stories make up this anthology.

Judges: Dan Bird, Lucy Luck, Vanessa Onwuemezi.

Readers: Emily Ajgan, Xanthi Barker, Jasmina Bidé, Rachel Brook, Ríbh Brownlee, Christina Carè, Emma Cheung, Ralitsa Chorbadzhiyska, Glenn Collins, Emily Cornell, Ruby Cowling, Olly Crabb, Leti Desbiere Batista, Kate Ellis, Lucy Fitzwilliam-Lay, Harry Gallon, Harriet Hirshman, Bret Johnson, Joe Johnston, Aysel Dilara Kasap, Laura Kenwright, Romla Kadir, Liam Konemann, Sarah Lambert, Cat Madden, Misha Manani, Stevie Marsden, Elliot Martin, Jarred McGinnis, Kira McPherson, Trisha Mendiratta, Kirat Pawar, Sophia Pearson, Melody Razak, Lucie Riddell, Jo Russell, Oscar Tapper, Ishita Uppadhayay, Billie Walker, Olivia Warren and Nikita Zankar. Especially the second- and third-round readers for their engagement and thoughtful feedback.

Polly Jones, Olly Crabb and Jo Russell for being the best Short Story Prize team and ensuring the competition runs smoothly.

Bret Johnson for his work on social media.

Denise Jones for her foreword and support.

Sue Tyley, our invaluable copy-editor and proofreader.

Our indie bookshop stockists.

Everyone who bought and read the 2019, 2020, 2021, 2022 and 2023 anthologies.

Our partners Spread the Word, Scratch Books, Prototype Publishing and *The London Magazine*. Special thanks to Bobby Nayyar, Tom Conaghan, Jess Chandler and Katie Tobin.

Online listings: writers-online.co.uk, nawe.co.uk, mironline.org, duotrope.com, neonbooks.org.uk, aerogrammestudio.com, christopherfielden.com, pocketmags.com, shortstoryaward.co.uk and nothingintherulebook.com.

Goodreads reviewers.

London Writers' Café, especially Lisa Goll.

Clays printers.

Turnaround book distribution, especially Benjamin, Eleanor and Claire.

Brick Lane Bookshop customers for choosing to support an independent.

Last but definitely not least, massive thanks to all the Brick Lane Bookshop booksellers: Denise Jones, Polly Jones, Kalina Dimitrova, Glenn Collins, Bret Johnson, Jo Russell and Olly Crabb for their hard work keeping the shop so busy and brilliant.

Brick Lane Bookshop has been
publishing annual short-story
anthologies since 2019.

166 | Brick Lane Bookshop | 166

Brick Lane Bookshop

Brick Lane Bookshop is a proudly independent bookshop, established in East London in 1978.

We're open every day from 10 a.m. to 6 p.m., and stock a carefully curated range of fiction, non-fiction, London books, children's books, poetry, essays, feminism, travel, classics, philosophy, foreign language books, cards, gifts, our iconic tote bags and more. We were named London's Independent Bookshop of the Year at the 2024 British Book Awards, a title we are delighted to have received in the same year we celebrate our twentieth anniversary on Brick Lane.

Our current projects and events include:
- Brick Lane Bookshop Short Story Prize
- Vibrant series of monthly author talks
- BLB Podcast
- BLB Press
- School outreach programme
- Young Readers' Fund
- East End Writers' Workshop
- Reading East London reading group
- Historical walking tours
- BLB independent publishing subscription

Visit our website and online shop at www.bricklanebookshop.org.

the blb

Issue 01 of *the blb* is now available, in store and online.

the blb is Brick Lane Bookshop's latest publishing project, a literary newsletter featuring book reviews, essays, poetry and short fiction. The newsletter extends the bookshop's tradition of encouraging new writers and promoting new and diverse voices. Whether you are fascinated by contemporary or classic literature, *the blb* is a new home for your writing.

For more information, updates on open calls and submission guidelines, you can follow BLB Press on Instagram @blb_press.

BLB Subscription

If you enjoyed this anthology and would like to receive more great books from independent publishers, sign up for the Brick Lane Bookshop subscription!

Our subscription service spotlights independent publishers who are making waves in literary fiction and non-fiction.

Sign up for 3 months, 6 months or a year and enjoy:
- A monthly new paperback release, hand picked by our booksellers
- Fully recyclable packaging
- The option of home delivery or in-store collection
- A limited-edition coloured Brick Lane Bookshoptote bag

One of our past subscribers said:

'I've always been a bit dubious of book subscriptions before because I'm picky about what I read and didn't like the thought of giving up control to someone else. But my thoughts have changed! [I've received] books from independent publishers I wouldn't have necessarily bought before. It's been a lovely surprise.'

Find out more at:
www.bricklanebookshop.org/subscriptions/.

BLB Podcast

The BLB Podcast celebrates and interrogates the short-story form. For each episode, we invite a writer to read from and discuss their work. We ask about their writing and editing processes, getting published and what they're reading.

Hosted, produced and edited by Kate Ellis and Peter J. Coles.

Find us at www.bricklanebookshop.org, or search 'Brick Lane Bookshop' on Spotify, Apple Podcasts or Pocket Casts.

Guests so far:

Isha Karki	Vanessa Onwuemezi
Aoife Inman	Keith Ridgway
Jarred McGinnis	Irenosen Okojie
Jem Calder	Manuel Muñoz
Wendy Erskine	Gurnaik Johal
Leon Craig	Imogen Fox
Niamh Mulvey	Jess Walter
Huma Qureshi	Eley Williams
Ben Pester	K. Lockwood Jefford